Mommie Dearest

An Andy Eastman novel

Dennis Berry

murderprose.com

Cover design: Lauren Modica

Cover illustration: *View to the South,* a 1987 watercolor by Alan C. ("Cal") Woolley, a gift from the artist to the author, gratefully used with permission of the estate.

MurderProse logo created by: *ideas@markaller.com*

Library of Congress Cataloguing-in-Publication Data:
Berry, Dennis

Mommie Dearest, an Andy Eastman novel/Dennis Berry

ISBN-13: 978-1463734381
ISBN-10: 1463734387

Murder, Kidnapping, Crime prevention, Citizen participation—Fiction.
Washington (State)—Seattle, Bainbridge Island, Olympic Peninsula.

2011 CreateSpace Trade Paperback Edition
Also available as an ebook.

Printed in the United States of America

http://www.murderprose.com
http://www.dennis-berry.com

For Steve, Cat, Karen, and Eric

And always, for Liz

Acknowledgements

To friends and former colleagues at The Boeing Company,
none of whom are accurately portrayed in this story:
thanks for your unwitting inspiration.

To cherished friends on Bainbridge Island, Puget Sound's Emerald
Isle: thanks for your constant stimulation and encouragement,
but mostly for your continuing friendship.

To Hazel Dawkins, dear friend and sometimes partner in literary crime:
thanks for your insightful reading of the story and many
helpful suggestions for improvement.

Eternal thanks to Elizabeth Berry, for her undying encouragement.

Errors, as always, are the responsibility of the author.

Mommie Dearest

An Andy Eastman novel

Think you know what happened on Bainbridge Island in June 2002?

Read on. Here's the whole story.

1

Em's Post-it note was still stuck to the phone, just where I had found it last night. A six-pack of beer hadn't improved its message:

> I've left, Andy. I don't
> know what I want, but I don't
> want this.
>   I could have waited until
> you got home, but it's better
> this way. I'd just say what I
> always say, and you'd still not
> hear me.
>   So good-bye. I'm going to
> think about my life and my
> future. Maybe you'll do the
> same. Or maybe not.
>
>   —Em

I dropped an expiring Camel into one of the empty beer cans and lighted another, the last in the pack. The pack had been full when I got home last night, pleased my vacation had finally arrived. I hadn't seen Em's note immediately and was surprised she wasn't home. But our old Audi wasn't parked outside and I figured she had gone out to pick up a few things before her trip to the San Juan Islands in the morning.

We had planned separate vacations this year. I would work on my story and Em would spend time with Alice Sharp, her dearest friend from their four-year occupation of Berkeley. Meanwhile Rick, our 15-year-old son, would be enjoying a two-week survival camp near Bend, Oregon with Alice's son, Miguel.

An hour later, Em hadn't returned and I began to wonder. Alice must have arrived from Portland sooner than expected and the two of them had taken off for the San Juan Islands early. Odd that Em didn't leave a note. So I went looking for one and found it stuck to the phone on the kitchen eating bar.

Now, six beers, twenty-one cigarettes, and eight sleepless hours later, the note still glared its mute accusation, and I still didn't know what to do about it. Maybe nothing? Ignore it and let Em return home, contrite and apologetic? Right. Dream on, Andy.

Finally, an epiphany. The note was in Em's handwriting, but her mother's fingerprints were all over it. Sylvia Hargrove disliked me with the intensity of a mother-in-law convinced that hardly anyone was good enough for Emily Hargrove, daughter of the landed Hargroves of Aberdeen, South Dakota. Least of all me.

The landed Hargroves' wealth derived from early adoption of the next big thing in cattle: South Dakota's first automated cattle feedlot, now twenty-five years old and still the largest. Every year, 110,000 head of brain-dead beef on the hoof grew up and out, their snouts poised above the Hargrove's food conveyers, noshing pelletized feed enriched with an ever-evolving mix of vitamins, minerals, growth hormones, and supplemental fiber. All that unruly grass that used to dominate the great plains of the great middle west had been plowed under and converted to vast fields of single-species seeds and grains easy to harvest and convert into feed pellets, corn syrup and ethanol. So much more tidy and efficient than having disorganized gaggles of contented bovinity roaming about and grazing; better to pack them into feedlots and monitor them as they ate from sunup to sundown, all day, every day, their days carefully numbered.

Here's the gist of 16 years of the Widow Hargrove's comments about her daughter's choice of husbands: "Ander Eastman will never amount to anything, Emily. You could have done so much better."

I probably hadn't gotten off on the right foot with my future mother-in-law when she gave me the grand tour of their feedlot, which included a close-up look at their Herefords and the automated feed conveyers that pushed steady streams of cattle kibble to millions of semi-ambulatory hamburgers, all of whom were sleepily doing their part: chowing down. While simultaneously spewing copious streams of crap I was attempting to dodge, with spotty success.

"So this is what money smells like," I'd quipped, sealing my doom.

I folded Em's note in half, rolled it into a tight little cylinder and jammed it through the opening of a dead beer can, slicing the tip of my finger in the process.

The phone rang. My "Hello" was a bit muffled by the bloody fingertip in my mouth.

"Andy? That you?"

"Mmm," I said, "Yeah."

"Jane Crawford, Andy. I need to talk to you right away."

"So talk already." I examined my finger. The bleeding seemed to have stopped, but it still hurt like hell. I'd probably survive.

"Not on the phone," Jane said. "I do this on the phone."

We agreed to meet at Pegasus, a coffee shop in Winslow, at eight o'clock, an hour from now. I hung up, wondering what would make Jane call me. Why me? Why not Em? Oh, well, I needed coffee anyway.

In the bathroom, I siphoned off another half-pint of minimally processed beer, then returned to the kitchen, filled the coffee-maker with ice-water from the fridge and added four scoops of Pegasus' Italian roast to a new filter. I would need something besides the vague promise of coffee an hour from now to take the edge off my headache and get me going, and nothing worked quite as well as Pegasus' darkest roast, laced with caffeine, my second-most favorite drug of choice.

I found a new pack of Camels in a dampish carton that shared the refrigerator's vegetable crisper with something that resembled a head of lettuce—it was green, anyway. I fired up a very cold cigarette as I went down the stairs to get the *Seattle Post-Intelligencer.* Our paperboy refuses to climb the 20 steps from the concrete boardwalk to our deck and, as usual, had "accidentally" missed the delivery tube designed to protect the *PI* from the elements.

The paper lay in a heap at the foot of the steps, but Mother Nature had fooled him this morning. The weather was clear and dry, warm for June, virtually windless. One of those days we keep secret, to deter Californication. Almost beautiful enough to distract me from my sputtering marriage.

I read the *PI's* front page as I climbed back up the steps to the house. The Mariners had swept a three-game series at New York, perhaps a harbinger of a better year? Perhaps we could hope to be competitive for the American League championship again? We must never give up hope, just because Ken Griffey did a couple years ago, seeking a greener pasture...er, center field in Cincinnati.

Boeing's layoffs at the commercial factories in Everett and Renton were nearly complete, the *PI's* aerospace columnist said, noting that commercial sales were slowly increasing, now that some airlines were showing signs they might survive 9-11 after all. In the meantime, Boeing's profits from the military side were spiking, thanks to the continuing war on terrorism. Ill winds and silver linings, and all that.

Washington's still-popular Chinese-American governor was still trying to find a way to balance the state's diminished budget, without alienating too much of his political base.

Meanwhile, the war on terrorism itself seemed to be in a momentary lull, everyone's attention focused on the intractable situation in the middle east, with daily suicide bombings and reprisals in Israel, and how, oh, how, would it all end. One writer of a letter to the editor likened the addictive hate-fest between Israelis and Palestinians to alcoholism, suggesting the conflict wouldn't end until everyone hit bottom and woke up some morning with their heads in the gutter. Unless they bled out first.

All in all, your average news day.

I interrupted the passionate gurgling of the coffee-maker long enough to fill a mug and brought the mug and the *PI* out onto the deck. The view of Seattle's skyline across the Sound was glorious, as always, five serene miles of deep blue waters that kept troubles at bay and riffraff away. This was why we lived on Bainbridge Island. It was worth every penny we had paid for the place. It was even worth commuting two and a half hours a day to a Boeing building well south of Seattle. At least when I got home at the end of a long day, I was someplace I wanted to be. My fellow tech writers thought me crazy, being a slave to a ferry schedule. Little did they know, little did they know.

Settling onto the chaise lounge, I checked my horoscope.

A member of the opposite sex offers an unexpected proposition. Proceed carefully.

Half right. How about *two* unexpected propositions from the fairer sex: one by phone, one by yellow sticky note?

I arrived at Pegasus at 7:55, just as Jonathan was unlocking the door.

"Be a few minutes before the coffee's ready, Andy," he said. "You're up awful early for someone on vacation. Aren't you off for a couple weeks?"

"Right, my vacation, such as it is. No rush for the coffee. I'll be out here," I said, gesturing towards the small patio at the side of the building. "I'll have a smoke while I wait for Mommie Dearest."

Jonathan grinned. Like everyone in our crowd, most everyone had a nickname. Jane Crawford's, for obvious reasons, was "Mommie Dearest." Jonathan's was "Jon," because he'd made it clear that he detested it.

Mine was "Andy." I liked "Andy," a good all-American name for a kid named Ander Eastman to commemorate a Swedish great-grandfather named Ander Östman ("Öst" being Swedish for "East," the family name forever altered by a hard-of-hearing Ellis Island immigration functionary) and also a noteworthy English predecessor: Andrew, the fourth Earl of someplace dank and moldy, whose family name, oddly enough, was Estmund. Someday I'll have to check out the fascinating and no doubt illuminating connections between the Östmans and the Estmunds—when I develop an old man's obsession with genealogy. Yeah, right.

"So where's your real 'Mommie Dearest?'" Jonathan said.

"In the San Juans, with her friend, Alice Sharp. Have you met Alice? Looks a little like Rita Moreno."

"Rita Moreno…Rita Moreno…why is that name familiar?"

Sometimes I forgot how young Jonathan was. "She was the Puerto Rican gal in "West Side Story." I warbled a few lines of "America":

"I like to be in A–mer–i–ca,

"Okay by me in A–mer–i–ca,

"Everything free in A–mer–i–ca…"

Jonathon chimed in. "'For a small fee in A–mer–i–ca.' You're right, I would have remembered meeting someone as hot as Rita Moreno."

"Anyway, Em and Alice are staying at a bed and breakfast up there. On Orcas, I think." I hoped.

"Good for her. So why aren't you with her? Oh dear, wait a minute. Separate vacations? Bad sign, Andy. Starts with little things like toilet seats left up and disputes over innie and outie toilet paper, moves right on into separate vacations and winds up with arguments about over-due child support. I'll bet Em's friend's divorced, right?"

I nodded.

Watch out, Andy. They're plotting strategy."

"Nothing like that, Jon." Christ, was he psychic? "Em just wanted to spend some time with Alice, and Alice had already paid for a B&B and invited her along. Besides, this way I'll have time to get some writing done."

"Okay, whatever you say. Hey, you gonna do your writing here at Pegasus? Cool. I've heard of some famous writer working out of the coffee shop at the Beverly Hills Hotel, but Pegasus? That's cool. Gonna put me in your book?"

"Sure, Jon. Every story needs some comic relief." It was a good enough exit line, so I stepped outside just in time to see Jane Crawford lurch her Expedition into the lot across the street. She seemed preoccupied as she emerged from the beast, staring at the ground as if seeking a message spelled out in cracked asphalt and oil stains.

"Meet you inside, Jane," I called out. To her face, we never called Jane Crawford "Mommie Dearest."

Jane looked up. "Oh! Oh hi, Andy. Be right there." She hurried into the coffee house, managing to make the walk into Pegasus appear illicit. Jonathan noticed.

I met Jane at the counter and Jonathan handed us our coffees while trying to leer at me. Jane and I took our cups out to the patio, where we could talk privately and where I could finally have my cigarette. We sat on a bench at the far corner of the patio. Jane watched me light up before speaking. She didn't seem to know what to say or how to start.

"So," I prompted. "What's up?"

"What would you do, Andy, if you wanted to find out what someone was doing when he's not around?"

The question caught me off guard. "Ask him? That would work? Why? Who are we talking about?"

She took a deep breath and looked away. It was easier for her to talk to the tree in the center of the patio. "Dan. It's Dan. You know that he lost his job at Boeing?" She glanced at me, then back at the tree. In fact, I didn't know that, although I had heard rumors of something less than honorable happening in Boeing's legal department, but rumors always fly fast at Boeing, much faster than any of their planes.

"For the last couple of months, he's been acting…I don't know…secretive, I guess. He still goes off on the ferry every morning. Says he's seeing people about new 'possibilities.' Positions with law firms, I guess. But he never really tells me anything, and sometimes he's gone overnight without any explanation and now he's hasn't been home for three days and I haven't heard from him and there's no reason I can think of for him to be gone and I'm worried sick." She paused to draw a breath. "So how can I find out what's really going on."

She stared straight into my eyes. "I'm worried, Andy. I'm really worried. This isn't like Dan at all and I don't know what to do. What *can* I do? Can you help me?"

What was I supposed to say? I certainly didn't know where Dan might be or what he might be doing, or—I hated to think it—with whom he might be doing it. Certainly wouldn't be the first time a laid-off middle-aged male had sought reassurance and comfort outside the marriage bed. But I knew nothing. Until just now I didn't even know he wasn't at Boeing any more. All I knew for sure was that I couldn't get involved in what sounded like a ticklish situation. Sure, Dan and I were friends, but I was hardly qualified to be a marriage counselor. Just ask Em.

Dan Crawford and I had been classmates at the University of Minnesota in an earlier millennium, cadets together in Air Force ROTC until Dan got sick of wearing his Air Force blues every Monday and especially weary of marching around inside the Armory building. He flushed Rot-see at the end of our freshman year and turned his full attention to his pre-law coursework. I stuck with AFROTC to the end, getting my degree in forestry and my commission in the Air Force on the same day at the end of the 60's, just as the Vietnam war was getting interesting. At that point, Dan and I lost touch, though I knew he was going on to get his Juris Doctor, followed by what I assumed would be a lucrative career in corporate law. Meanwhile, I was gathering and feeding intelligence to brass and silver-encrusted bosses who knew exactly what to do with intelligence that failed to jibe with the official view about how US forces were routing the enemy: ignore it; if possible, bury it.

Eventually, Dan's career path and mine merged at Boeing, where I was hired a technical writer, Dan as a negotiator of government contracts. Both of us happened to have chosen Bainbridge Island as home, and our friendship had grown since the day seven years ago when our shopping carts had collided at Town and Country Thriftway. Jane and Em had become friends as well, and our Rick and their Dan Junior, the same age as Rick, were classmates in Bainbridge's schools; they'd start high school in the fall.

Last year I'd helped Dan Junior rescue one of his friends, a sexually confused kid who had fled the horrors of home only to experience the horrors of Seattle's First Avenue. Dan Junior, Rick and I had found the kid quickly by scouting the most likely places and the three of us persuaded the boy to return home. The kid was doing much better these days, thanks to some intensive counseling by a good therapist, perhaps aided by my own "come to Jesus" counseling of the boy's stepfather, who had no trouble grasping my meaning when I told him he'd lose his private parts if he ever touched his stepson's again. A week later the guy split, and by now has probably found another unattached female with a young son. I should have turned the creep over to the cops.

Maybe Jane had heard of my "rep" for locating missing persons.

Except Dan Senior wasn't some confused teenager, and I didn't want to be involved in his life as anything more than a friend. Especially now. My wife had just left me, for Christ's sake, and I had two weeks of book-writing "vacation" in front of me, and I needed to do some serious soul-searching and accomplish some even more difficult behavior modification if I had any hope of enticing back the woman I loved. The last thing I needed was to try and solve Dan and Jane's marital problems; I wasn't doing that well on my own.

I needed to break the news to Mommie Dearest gently. I grasped both of Jane's hands in mine, looked reassuringly into her eyes and spoke calmly and softly, yet determinedly.

"Of course, Jane. I'll do whatever I can."

The fly paper made no noise as it unfurled, and it barely held me back as I walked Jane to her car.

2

Alongside her car, Mommie Dearest tried to fill in some blanks, without much success. No, she didn't know if Dan had taken any airplane trips lately. No, she didn't handle the bills, not even the phone bill, so she knew of no unusual outgoing phone calls. Yes, she had received a couple calls for Dan from a "Mister Smith," but that was about it.

We agreed that when Dan showed up, she would invite me for dinner so I could judge his behavior and state of mind for myself. Right. My pot was so well-qualified to call Dan Crawford's kettle black.

Before she drove away, we talked about our kids. Dan Junior would be attending a sailing school on Seattle's Lake Washington later in the summer, and Jane was interested to hear about Rick's choice of summer diversions, a hard-working, two-week camp in the wilderness of eastern Oregon, led by a hard-talking, ex-Marine drill-master with a hard-nosed attitude about the necessity of kids learning wilderness survival skills to be prepared for the "big one." I was pretty sure the drill sergeant could probably bring about the "big one" by sheer determination, and he'd found a ready recruit in Rick, whose interest in such things both thrilled and terrified me. Thrilled, because any father wants his son to be manly and self-sufficient; terrified, at the potential consequences.

Over the last couple years, Rick and I have had several long talks about self-preparedness and self-defense, and especially about weapons. Rick understood my view—guns don't kill people; people with guns kill people. Rick's view was more reasoned. He wanted to learn about weaponry so he could take care of himself in any situation. We seemed destined to discuss this subject the rest of our lives, both of us convinced of the rightness of our views, neither of us willing to yield—until this summer.

When I agreed that Rick could go to camp in Oregon, I hoped he would interpret that as proof that I respected his opinion, trusted his judgment, and felt it was good for him to explore his beliefs. I didn't have to say that to him, but of course I did anyway. I did not tell him that I hoped he would develop blisters from the straps on his backpack and come home before he got into trouble.

Now, after internalizing Em's "I've had it!" departure note, I was relieved that Rick wasn't around to observe me morph into a better man, especially since I no clue how to attempt that. It wouldn't be pretty. It might not work.

At home, the blinking red light on the answering machine announced two messages, the first from Jane's missing hubby, Dan.

"Jane tells me you are to be our dinner companion tonight, Andy. I'll look forward to it. See you at seven."

The second message was from Jane herself, confirming the dinner date. She sounded nervous.

I was too. The evening wasn't going to be much fun. Dan would be on guard, Jane would be on edge, and I would be too preoccupied with my own troubles to help them sort through theirs.

Crap. How do I get myself into these things? At best, I would be a battered line judge evaluating acrimonious matrimonial volleys. At worst? I wouldn't think about "worst."

A bottle of Henry Weinhard's Private Reserve Ale from the refrigerator accompanied me to the deck—a liquid lunch *alfresco*. What I needed to do was to starve myself all day, then gorge myself at their table, grunting as much as possible. I would keep my mouth too full to engage in conversation. They would never invite me back, which sounded good to me. I would not get involved.

There are three, not two, things you never discuss with other people—religion, politics, and most importantly, marriage—especially yours and theirs. That little voice that tells you it's time to *Run away! Run away!?* Mine was screaming its little lungs out.

So I drank my beer, considered other options (none), and dozed off in the sun. Frustration and Henry's Ale do that to me, the better to convert simple carbohydrates to waistline inches without interference from an active metabolism. I didn't awaken until the first drops of icy rain spattered my face.

Inside, I watched the sudden squall chase sailboats towards Shilshole Marina across the expanse of water, grabbing my binoculars for a closer look. A few sloops didn't make it around the marina's breakwater. After the squall passed, seven or eight of them managed to right themselves and wobble limply into port. A Coast Guard cutter was steaming toward the two who didn't.

Maybe the Coast Guard would retrieve me tonight when I got in over my head.

To my surprise, the evening started out great. Jane's steak Dianne was as juicy as the goddess herself. Dan, talkative and outwardly happy, reminisced about our good old Rot-see days of close-order drill in the U's Armory and trying to keep in step with our more coordinated compatriots. Hut-one-hut-two…skip-skip, hut-one-hut-two-skip, trip. Pathetic.

Even Mommie Dearest finally relaxed, then stiffened a bit as I finally made a inquiry that could qualify as responding to Jane's request.

"So how does it feel to not have a paycheck anymore, Dan?"

"Surprisingly good. Boeing gave me sort of a pewter parachute. Not the gold one the CEO will get when he finally retires, but not a tin cup either. I tell you, getting half a year's salary all at once is pretty nice. With what we've got set aside, we're okay."

"Good for you. If they laid me off, I'd have just enough money to make it home. Anything else on your plate yet? You're way too young to retire."

A damp finger in the air could have sensed the drop in temperature. Dan's relaxed face turned sour, eyebrows thickened, lips compressed into razors. "Nothing definite. But I've got some options. Some firms in town are interested because of my government contacts and work as a negotiator."

I tried to look grateful at being taken into his confidence and nodded for him to continue. His demeanor improved a bit as he mentioned a couple law firms I knew of. Both were in the Norton Building near the Seattle ferry terminal. I reminded them of my experience a few years back, when I lost my shirt in an attempt to go free-lance as a legal and engineering writer. I had rented space on the second floor of the Norton Building, where rents were comparatively cheap. The law firms

Dan mentioned were on the higher-priced upper floors, and I'd lob-
bied both of them to drum up some business—unsuccessfully.

I wondered to myself if I should contact them again, just to verify
Dan's information. He seemed to read my mind.

"Just don't go talking to them again, okay? They've already told
you 'no,' and if you mention we're friends, you'll screw up my chances
for sure."

He chuckled. "Kidding, Andy. Just yanking your chain. Anyway,
I've been thinking it might be time to do something completely different. Maybe teach law. At Gonzaga in Spokane."

Jane groaned. When you're accustomed to the marine temperate-
ness and lush greenery of western Washington, eastern Washington's
Palouse country, endless rolling field of wheat, looms immense, and
immensely bleak and barren—boiling in the summer, wind-blown and
frigid in the winter.

Dan back-peddled. "Or maybe right here at the U-Dub." Jane still
looked unsure.

On the whole, Dan sounded convincing—a little too convincing,
with just enough name-dropping for his story to be believable. Whatever, all of it was news to Jane; he'd told her little about his plans. I
wondered why.

A moment later I knew Dan was being less than truthful, even for
a lawyer. "Maybe I'll go back to school and get my MBA."

That, I just couldn't believe, not after all our lambasting of
Reagan- and Bush-era MBAs and their insufferably simplistic scenarios
for instant corporate revitalization, scenarios that invariable involved
copious bean counting (MBA buzz-word: "metrics") and inevitable
out-sourcing, invariably stifling whatever creativity and productivity the
remaining managers and workers could muster while clinging to their
jobs.

"You're not serious, Dan."

"Absolutely. With an MBA on top of my JD…"

"…You'd be a total jerk."

Dan's smile was a bit too self-satisfied for my taste, but I smiled
anyway. Jane chuckled as she headed into the kitchen to make a pot of
coffee. A half-pound of Pegasus's Italian roast had been my contribu-
tion to the feast.

Alone with Dan, I tried to appear both relaxed and trustworthy,
hoping the smile on my face would tell Dan, *"See? I'm your friend. You
know you can tell me anything and it will stay just between us very good friends."*

I couldn't read the look on Dan's face, but he didn't seem eager to fess up to anything.

"Well," I said, preparing my retreat, "I'll see if Mommie Dearest needs any help."

He snagged my sleeve. "Tell Jane not to worry, Andy. Tell her everything is under control and whatever happens, she and the kids—all of us—will be okay."

So he knew why I'd been invited to dinner. I felt embarrassed. And I know I was tired. Still, my reaction caught me by surprise.

"Look, Dan. I don't know what's going on and, personally, I don't give a damn. I'm here only because Jane asked me to find out what was happening with you. She's worried. She says you're never home. She's afraid you're in trouble. So don't tell me, don't you *dare* tell *me*—to tell *her*, for Christ's sake—that 'everything is under control.' Just what the hell does that mean, counselor?"

I finally remembered the maxim of whoever it was that said, 'Very little learning occurs when one's mouth is open.'

My mouth, and Dan's, remained closed for awhile.

Finally Dan spoke, haltingly. "Jane can't know—I'm getting things set up that should work out very well...." He raised his hand to stifle the interruption he saw coming.

"That's really all I can say about it, except the whole deal is sensitive, Andy, really tricky. Delicate. I *have* been preoccupied lately, maybe even a little mysterious. When you talk to Jane—if you would do that—please tell her that. It will all be over in a couple of days, then there won't be all this secrecy. And yeah, I know I ought to be able to tell her that myself. I do know I should do that. But I'm afraid if I tell her too much, too soon, then things might not turn out okay, not okay at all. So please, as a favor to me, tell her that everything is okay. Because really, it is. At least, it soon will be."

I didn't know what could be so delicate that Dan felt compelled to keep it hidden from his wife. But what really bothered me, and I don't think Dan was aware of it, was the look on his face as he was giving me all this desperate earnestness that didn't explain a damn thing.

Dan Crawford, Esquire, looked afraid. Petrified. Scared shitless. Neither his formidable training in law at Harvard nor his years of poker-faced dealing on Boeing's behalf could disguise the fearful bleakness in his eyes.

3

The next morning, another call from Jane Crawford summoned me back to her house. As usual, Dan had left early. As usual, he had been evasive about his plans. While Jane served coffee with strawberry shortcake left over from last night, I passed along Dan's message.

"He couldn't tell me that himself?"

"He said he was afraid he would tell you too much. For some reason he didn't want that. But it seemed to me that he was real concerned that you understand that everything would be all right for you guys and that you weren't to worry."

God, Dan's explanation sounded as lame coming out of my mouth as it had from his. But no way was I going to tell Jane how fearful Dan had looked. No way. She would be more disturbed than I had been.

"I don't see why he doesn't trust me. When I asked him when he would be home tonight, he wouldn't say. Said he *couldn't* say, that it depended on how long his meetings lasted, that he'd call if he was delayed."

"That's progress."

"Is it? Still feels like he's sneaking off somewhere."

As unlikely as it seemed, I couldn't help wondering if another woman was in the picture. Like Em, Jane was everything a man could want in a woman. Loving, caring, utterly devoted. But you never know. Stress overwhelms and distorts. Like Em being overwhelmed by the stresses of trying to help me sort out what I would do if and when I ever grew up. Or Em finally agreeing with the Duchess of Dakota

Feedlots' assessment of my potential. Neither possibility was much fun to think about. Boy, does reality suck.

Boy, did I need a Camel. Jane followed me out on the deck, where I lit up. After awhile we strolled down to their dock, where their two boats were moored on opposite sides. One was a 36-foot fiberglass sloop, the Lady Jane, a graceful boat with a broad beam. But I preferred their classic 25-foot Chris-Craft speedboat, with its gleaming wood decking—mahogany? Probably. I suspected that Dan had spent more money restoring the speedboat than I earned in a year, even counting my free-lance writing, which hadn't added much to the Eastman family bottom line. Jane and I stepped aboard the Lady Jane and climbed down into the galley.

I love boats. I've always wanted one. I looked forward to the day I could afford one, say when I won a Lotto jackpot or got a nice advance for a novel. I still had hopes that could happen, that my agent in Seattle, Juanita Wardell, would find a publisher willing to take a chance. Completing one book and starting another helped a lot, Juanita maintained. I was demonstrating perseverance, she said, and publishers liked writers who weren't one-hitters. I hoped she was right. But I still bought tickets for the Wednesday and Saturday Lotto drawings, week after week. And the Mega-Millions mega-delusion on Tuesdays and Fridays, too.

While I admired the custom cabinets in the Lady Jane's galley, Jane lighted the diesel-fueled stove and heated water for coffee. Aboard the boat she made coffee the old fashioned way: coarsely-ground beans dumped into cold water brought to a quick, hard boil, then steeped for five minutes. That was the way my maternal grandmother had made coffee, preferring the method she'd learned in Sweden to any "newfangled" percolator or drip machine. She wouldn't buy a Mr. Coffee if Joe DiMaggio spoke Swedish. The funny thing was that her coffee tasted better than Starbuck's—and a whole lot better than DiMaggio's. I'm absolutely sure my grandmother had never seen an actual coffee bean, just the coarse grit in cans of Folgers or Maxwell House.

So Jane and I sat and drank coffee in the boat, talking without actually saying much, interrupted only three times by her children, who were probably checking us out to make sure I wasn't making a pass at Jane. Just to make sure Jane wasn't fielding one. Fifteen-year-old Dan Junior stopped by first, asking when Rick would be back from camp in Oregon.

15

"As soon as he scores enough coups against the Indians, probably." Dan Junior looked pained. "A week from Friday," I clarified. Dan Junior left, shaking his head.

Jane's oldest, Richard, 17, ducked through the hatch to say he was taking the Volvo to Bremerton for servicing. A few moments later, 16-year-old Maria, who looks like Elizabeth Taylor looked in "American Velvet," poked her head in to say she would ride along with Richard.

At noon we hit low tide—the inlet's and our own—and ascended the now-steep gangplank from the floating dock to the upper walkway. Inside the house, Jane rummaged through the ancient roll-top desk in Dan's study until she found some recent bank statements and other papers that seemed to relate to finances. She apologized about knowing so little about their condition, money-wise.

"Dan always handles everything."

I knew that. Em did the same for us. That had, in fact, been the subject of a few heated discussions about our financial foibles over the years. In my family, Em wore the money belt. It didn't seem to fit me. Too constraining. Hmm. Another piece of our boy-meets-girl, boy-loses-girl marriage puzzle.

I promised Jane to return the papers right away. Then kept my word, making copies in town and hustling the originals back to Jane before heading home. No way was I going to let Dan catch me with my grubby, inept paws on his money belt.

All that coffee made me feel groggy, rather than lively. A nap seemed a wonderful idea. The phone awakened me a few minutes later.

"How're you coming on your story?" Juanita Wardell. My agent.

"Coming along. Taking shape."

"Good. Spell-check what you've finished and bring it and a synopsis to my office at 4:30 this afternoon."

"How come?"

"I want to read it before we meet with Chris Noble tomorrow. Chris is a senior editor from Wallingford Press."

"Oh, wow. Oh, shit, er, I mean, I can't make it this afternoon, Jaunita. I've got to pick up Em's car at the mechanic's."

"Really. Well, tomorrow then. I guess I don't need to see it before our meeting with Chris at Maximilien's in the Market. Bring the synopsis and whatever's completed, so we can show it to Chris. He's already read your first manuscript and says he likes it. Now, I think he's looking for proof that you're not a one-book wonder. I don't want to get your hopes up, Andy, but I think this could be our big chance."

I said I would get to Maximilien's before two tomorrow, then I hung up and shook like a dog coming in from a storm. Whoa. A real live editor wanted to meet me. Someone who actually liked my work. Maybe a future Chris-Craft could be more than an idle fantasy.

Abruptly, reality struck. I had nothing at all to show Chris Noble, Juanita, or anyone. Sure, I'd drafted a couple sketchy chapters and had completed a rough outline, but only in my head. It would take hours to put anything together for tomorrow.

But I could do it. I knew I could. I always worked better under a deadline. I climbed the stairs to the study and fired up my bulbous "Bondi-Blue" iMac.

While the machine beeped to life to tell me it would be ready to work when I was, the phone rang again.

"Hi, dad!" Rick said. "Guess what?"

I didn't dare. Was he wounded?

"We're coming home. Tomorrow. This place sucks kitty litter through a straw. It's a hundred and ninety degrees and we've been sitting here in our teepees of day-glo plastic, just like original Native Americans used, tying sheep-shanks and bow-lines for two days. Our leader is the original boy scout, dad. And he confiscated my *Playboy*, the Nazi. I think he's a fag."

"And?" I managed.

"So we're leaving tonight. Miguel and I snuck out this afternoon and we've already hitched into Bend. That's where I'm calling from. Boy, I'm glad you gave me that calling card. Miguel used his AmEx card for our bus tickets to Seattle. So we'll get in at nine tomorrow morning, and we should be able to catch the ten-ten boat to the island. Can you pick us up at the Winslow terminal?"

I argued with him long enough to gauge his determination, which was far greater and much better-planned than mine.

"Dad? Did I say that I called the main office for the camp and arranged a full refund of my tuition? Miguel's too?"

Clever, Rick, clever. "So, Miguel's coming, too, huh?" I didn't mind. They had been friends most of their lives, ever since Miguel and Rick had started kindergarten together at the Metropolitan Learning Center in Portland, at that time the only publicly funded "alternative" school in the country, where the kids weren't divided into K-6 classes by age group and grade level, but by subject interest and mastery. The boys had been new to the school as kindergartners. We'd just moved to Portland from northern California. Expat Alice and Miguel had just arrived from Mexico, where Miguel had been born and where his still-expatriate dad still lived, still manufacturing drug paraphernalia for what was still a determinedly stoned counterculture. Miguel's dad had remarried after Alice and Miguel left. His new wife spoke only Spanish, detested Alice, and barely tolerated Miguel during his not-so-*Feliz Navidad* annual visits with his dad.

"Yeah, Miguel's coming. That's okay, isn't it? I mean, it's his money that bought the tickets and all."

"Of course." Where else would he go? His mother was with Em. Presumably. Actually, it was more than okay. In that instant, I was delighted that Rick was coming home. So far, my vacation had been filled with my problems and Mommie Dearest's and Dan Crawford's, and I was woefully weary of feeling sorry for myself. My focus needed to change. I needed to get things on track. I needed to charge ahead.

And right now I needed to start getting on with my book. I looked forward to seeing both Rick and Miguel and had to bite my tongue to keep from telling Rick about the Wallingford editor. I'd save that for tomorrow.

And yeah, I was grateful that Rick had secured the tuition refund and that Miguel had the means to buy their bus tickets. Of course, Miguel would always have money. His mother's parent's only grandchild, he would eventually inherit several thousand acres of Napa Valley vineyards, prime graperage purchased shortly after Miguel's grandfather made several dozen million dollars by inventing some widget indispensable to several dozen million Windows-based PCs. I never found out what that widget did, exactly, but it sure bought many, many acres of first-class vineyards.

One of the nicest things about the boys' friendship was that Miguel's future wealth never seemed to get in the way. I had always given Rick the credit for that, for his largeness of spirit and lack of covetousness. On the other hand, maybe Miguel had already endowed Rick with a numbered account in Switzerland.

On that happy thought, I turned to the task at hand—eagerly.

Four hours later, I had finished three pretty fair short chapters and polished off a two-page synopsis of the new book. Together with the first book, I envisioned they would create a whole new genre encompassing elements of both horror and mystery. That's me—Edgar Allen Doyle, Arthur Conan Poe—take your pick. I could just see it. After reading my sample chapters and synopsis, Wallingford's Chris Noble would eagerly cough up the big bucks.

And Em would come crawling back. Well hey, this was *my* fantasy, which are rarely constrained by logic—and never, ever by political correctness.

I met the boys' ferry in Winslow the next morning, bought them waffles and bacon at the Streamliner Diner, told them about my upcoming meeting with the editor from Wallingford, and heard their stories about the nights of the Nazi and entrapment by bowline and sheepshank. After delivering the boys to the house, I returned to town, left my old VW Rabbit illegally parked in the Thriftway parking lot, and walked down to the ferry terminal. In Seattle, I walked up 1st Avenue to Pike Place Market, making it to Maximilien's at 1:45. Juanita Wardell had already secured a table with a view of Elliott Bay and, bless her heart, had already ordered two margaritas.

"To success," she said, raising her glass. "At last."

"To mutual success," I added. "May it continue."

Juanita said Chris Noble's plane had landed and he would be arriving in about 45 minutes. In town to promote another writer's new release, Juanita had snagged him with the promise of a late lunch. They had met three months earlier at the American Bookseller's convention in Anaheim, California, where he had agreed to read my first manuscript. Two months later, he had called back, moderately enthusiastic.

"You never mentioned that."

"I try not to talk about things that 'may' happen, Andy. No point in getting your hopes up. But now...."

"We're beyond 'maybe?'"

"That's my sense of it. I think Chris may be ready to offer a contract if he likes what he sees today. You did bring the sample chapters and synopsis, didn't you? I want to send them with Chris."

I handed them over. She scanned the synopsis, then read the first chapters, more slowly. To my surprise and delight, she had tears in her eyes when she looked up.

"This is beautiful, Andy. Good, really good. Better than anything else you've written. If Chris Noble doesn't buy this, I need to find another line of work."

I muttered my thanks just as Noble was escorted to our table by the *maitre d'*. Noble was short, nearly bald, and well-tanned, a bespectacled man with bright eyes illuminating an otherwise unremarkable face. A monk's tonsure of crisp black hair encircled his perfectly round bald spot.

Juanita introduced me, then handed him the second book's synopsis. "I know you don't usually read an author's work in front of him, Chris, but I wanted you to see what the next book looks like—proof positive that there is indeed a second book. You'll see Andy's tied up the loose ends of the first story and added some new elements that will lead naturally to a much longer series."

Noble studied the two-page synopsis carefully. He nodded his head, apparently at things he liked and raised his eyebrows at things that surprised him, probably the same things that had surprised me when I wrote them yesterday.

"Okay. Looks promising. Sample chapters?" Juanita handed them over. "I usually don't do this, but I have to say I'm intrigued."

After reading the three chapters—just twenty pages, Noble just sat there holding the pages for a moment, shifting his gaze to the bouquet of pink roses in the center of our table. Wordlessly, he rose, left the table and headed for the exit. I don't know what Juanita was thinking, but I was shattered. My writing had never caused a walkout, but apparently not even the promise of a free lunch could keep Chris Noble at the table after being exposed to such drivel.

My appetite was gone. But a drink, I could manage a drink. A big strong one. A whole bottle of tequila, the bleached worms at the bottom all the lunch I needed, or deserved. I waved at the waiter and ordered another margarita for Juanita and two for me.

Chris Noble returned just as our drinks arrived. He picked up one of my margaritas and drank half of it.

"Sorry. I needed to make a phone call before everyone had gone home for the day." He shook my hand. "We want to publish you, Andy."

I think I said something, maybe "Thank you?" More probably, "Uh…."

"Andy, Wallingford will publish both of your books. I just spoke with Jack Mackey, our publisher, and he agrees with my assessment of your talent and your salability."

I remained speechless. Juanita filled the void. "Should we adjourn to my office, or would you like to discuss the contract now?"

Noble glanced at me before looking at Juanita, his eyebrows raised. "Here would be good. My plane leaves at four-thirty. But…." He glanced at me and smiled.

"Of course," Juanita said, then turned to me. "Andy, Chris and I will be discussing the details of the contract, so it would be best if you took your leave now and let me earn my money. We'll talk later, okay?"

As a yet-unpublished novelist, I was eager to hear those "details," especially the advance I hoped they would be talking about, but Juanita was right: she was better-equipped and much more experienced than me. I held out my hand to Chris Noble. "I can't tell you how pleased I am that you like my work."

He stood up as he shook my hand. "I'm happy Juanita brought it to my attention. And I'm glad we had the chance to meet, Andy. I look forward to working with you as your editor."

I turned to Juanita then, almost incoherent with gratitude. "And thank you, Juanita. For everything. Everything."

"No, Andy. Thank *you*. If it wasn't for you, I wouldn't be here."

I suppose she was right, technically. But if it wasn't for Juanita, Chris Noble wouldn't know me from any other writer in the slush pile. For that matter, if it hadn't been for Juanita's prodding, there wouldn't have been anything to show Noble today.

I glanced back at their table as I reach the exit, to see if they'd started their negotiations. They hadn't. They were watching me. They both waved.

I floated down First Avenue toward the ferry terminal, hovering a foot or so above the sidewalk. After a block or so, I looked at my watch and fell to Earth and started running.

I caught the 3:00 boat, barely. Wow, my luck really was changing.

I felt like throwing my fist in the air in the general direction of South Dakota and yelling at the top of my lungs. "Suck on that, Sultana of Silage!"

Back at the house, Rick had left a note propped on the phone. He and Miguel had gone beachcombing at the south end of Rolling Bay Walk, toward Skiff Point. Rolling Bay Walk was the quaint but accurate name for our neighborhood, a quarter-mile of closely spaced houses connected by a sidewalk atop a seawall that protects the houses and provides access by foot. A few of the houses can be reached by car, too, like ours, at the far north end of the Walk, where a narrow access lane with the unlikely name of Gertie Johnson Road ends in a small parking lot next to the house. Another road approaches Rolling Bay Walk from its south end, and the sidewalk at that end is wide enough to drive on for a distance. A few of the houses on the south end of the walk even have garages.

Since Rick knew I was in Seattle for the big meeting, he had added a postscript to his note: "Let's eat out tonight to celebrate." My son, the positive thinker.

Yeah. That'd be fun. And it would also be fun to spread the news of my good fortune, so I made a few calls around the island. I thought of trying to call Em, too, but I could only guess where she might be staying, and neither of us had one of those new cellular phones. Instead, I mentally composed a new message for the answering machine that would tell Em to call me for "really good news."

As it would turn out, I would forget to record that new message for the answering machine, Em and I wouldn't talk for several days, and because of what would then be happening, my really good news would be the farthest thing from my mind.

But at that moment I could think only of imminent wealth and fame, and the party I would throw to celebrate both. I made some self-congratulatory phone calls to share the news with friends. To show you what kind of friends I have, only two of them asked for loans. To show you what dear friends we are, I laughed them off. The last of my dozen or so calls was to Mommie Dearest.

She said she was very happy for me. She didn't sound very happy for me, or for anyone else. "What's the matter, Jane?" She didn't respond. I repeated the question.

"Same thing. But now I know Dan's in trouble. He hasn't been home since yesterday morning and today he got two calls from men who wouldn't identify themselves. Two hours ago, a man who called himself 'Bob Smith' knocked on the door. He said he and Dan used to work together and he had some important questions to ask him. He gave me a card with only a phone number on it. He said Dan needed to call him right away."

"No name on the card?"

"Not his name, not even a company name. Just a phone number. And if that isn't weird enough, when I called the number, a woman answered by just repeating the number. She wouldn't identify herself. When I asked for Bob Smith, she said she would have him call me back. I told her not to bother."

"What's the number?"

She gave it to me and I wrote it on my note pad, with "Bob Smith?" written next to it. I told Jane I would find out what I could and made her promise to call me the minute she heard from Dan. I looked at the note pad again and saw where I had written the names of the Norton Building lawyers Dan had mentioned the other night. I looked at the clock. I could just catch the 4:35 boat to Seattle, if I rushed. That would put me at Seattle's Colman Dock just after five and at the Norton Building a few minutes later.

I could do that, but the lawyers would have already gone home, unless I called and asked them to wait. And how would I do that? "I wanted to ask you some embarrassing personal questions about one of your potential associates, Dan Crawford. What can you tell me?" Sure. Right. No lawyer wishing to remain a member of the bar would ever answer a question like that, certainly not on the phone.

I decided to wait until tomorrow and call on the law offices in person. Maybe that would give me time to dream up a plausible cover story. Yeah, tomorrow would be soon enough. Tonight, we would celebrate. I got myself another Henry's from the fridge to help myself plan the evening. The boys and I would go someplace nice. I still had a hundred dollars left on my Visa credit limit; we could use that. If we got carried away, there was always Miguel's Enriched Plutonium American Express card as backup.

Soon, I would be paying off my creditors. I might do so in person, just to see their incredulous looks. I wondered how long it would take to get my advance. Would there be one check for the advances on both books or one check for each? For how much? And when? Right away? So much to wonder about. What to buy first. Whom to pay off first. Where to take Em for a vacation, a real vacation—assuming she'd go with me. My fantasy was getting more real and more enjoyable by the minute.

I hadn't had such fun in years. I reclined on the chaise on the deck. The sky was turning that wonderful shade of gold the heavens reserve for special occasions. In an hour or two, the sun would set behind the house and its nearly horizontal rays would bounce off the windows of buildings across the Sound. For a moment, Seattle's skyline would appear to be on fire. In the meantime, I watched the ships steaming toward Elliott Bay, container ships, mostly, their towering stacks defying gravity. The wakes of the passing ships created overlapping, competing diamond-shaped waves that slip-slapped the base of the sea wall below the deck. A nice sound, like someone slapping hundred-dollar bills into my hands.

I sighed and closed my eyes and thought really nice thoughts for awhile. I must have slept for an hour or two, because the skies were dimmer when I awakened. I looked down the walkway to the south. The tide was in, nearly up to the sea-wall, almost completely covering the beach. What could be keeping the boys? They couldn't still be beach-combing. Most of the beach was under water. Where could they be?

I came fully awake when I heard the gunshot.

4

The sound of gunfire next to a large body of water is not particularly loud, and there's no echo whatsoever. The shot I heard wouldn't have been heard 'round the world, but it was utterly terrifying because it came from the south end of the walk, where Rick's note said he and Miguel had gone. I hurtled down the steps to the sidewalk and sprinted the sidewalk to its south end, out of breath long before I reached the parking lot. It had been years since my last quarter-mile dash. No, let's be honest. It had been decades since my last dash anywhere farther than the 15 feet between bed and toilet.

I couldn't see the boys. I called Rick's name but heard nothing louder than my own booming heartbeat. Despite the stitch in my left side and lungs that felt like (and probably smelled like) burlap bags of smoldering coals, I continued on, trying to pick up my pace.

Ka-thunggg. Another shot, louder, closer, but still farther south. I yelled Rick's name again as I raced around the big house at the south end of the parking lot and hurtled off the seawall onto a narrow strip of exposed sand and gravel at its base, all that remained of the beach at high tide. Toppling head-first into the detritus at the edge of the sea, I swallowed a good bit of a clam's all-you-can-eat buffet. My glasses flew off, but I found them after a little groping in the grunge. At least they hadn't broken.

I resembled the menopause version of the creature from the black lagoon as I staggered upright, gook in my hair, slime streaming off my face—a source of helpless amusement for Rick and Miguel, who stood a few feet above me on the seawall, doubled over in laughter. Dangling forgotten from Rick's left hand was his pride and joy, a pump-action .22-calibre rifle.

"I told you never to use that unless I'm around!"

To his credit, Rick managed to look chagrined. "I'm sorry, dad. We were real careful. We were shooting at some old cans at the foot of the bank, so the bullets wouldn't sail out over the water." He looked away then, and I could see he was having a real struggle not to laugh openly at this hippy-drippy apparition telling him to be careful. Looking away, he finished his apology. "I won't do it again, I promise."

From a standpoint of maintaining our father-son relationship, what had just transpired was probably all to the good. Had I caught him cold with the gun, without the preamble of my face-first exploration of the briny shallows, I would have been even more wrathful. That would have damaged Rick's emerging male ego in front of his best friend. At least that's what all the books say: criticize the act and not the actor—and always in private, not in public. Hard to remember that advice, but this time I did, mostly. For his part, Rick was trying to earn points by letting me preserve more paternal dignity than my appearance commanded.

Later I would see the humor in the situation and would be grateful that both of us had acted as we had. An angry confrontation then, especially about that subject—guns—would have been a horrible memory to live with in the coming days.

But at that moment I was more concerned with getting back to the house without being seen by all the neighbors. It would be tricky to explain. "Well, see, I'm getting this terrific advance from a publisher, so I thought I would celebrate with a feast of seaweed."

After a very hot, very long shower, we began our real celebration. The boys wanted to see a movie, the latest *Terminator*-ripoff playing in Seattle, so we ferried the Rabbit to Seattle and did that. Then we needed to eat. I didn't care what we ate, as long as it didn't grow up in the ocean. We stopped by a McDonalds' for their largest burgers and barrels of fries, then had strawberry shortcake at the Denny's near the south end of Lake Union. The lingering aftertaste of seaweed finally succumbed to gobs of strawberry-infused whipped cream.

I should say something about guns here, my feelings about them, as contrasted to Rick's. I don't like them. Pure and simple. It wasn't always so. As a kid deer hunting with his dad, I didn't feel that way.

When I was 13, my father determined I finally was old enough to join him in the annual quest for a white-tail buck. Not a female of the species; in those days, does were hunted only by poachers. We drove from Minneapolis to the terrain dad and my Uncle Leland had always favored, way up in the wilds of northern Minnesota, nearly into Canada, where the herd was relatively small in numbers and well spread out, but where deer still far outnumbered hunters, so the likelihood of getting bagged by a drunken weekend warrior was minimal. To my amazement, even more than dad's, I got my deer in my first year as a red-blooded gun-toting American male. But the cost....

A white-tailed buck, three prongs on either side, eased out of the brush and stood, head raised, sniffing the air, less than fifty yards from me. I had been sitting nearly immobile on a stump, freezing, waiting for dad and Leland to complete their searching circuit of the surrounding hills and drive any deer toward me and my cousin Joe, who was sitting on another stump on the other side of the little knoll between us. It's hard to say who was more surprised, the young buck on my side of the hill, who stood there in plain sight, smelling his enemy—or the young buck on the stump holding a rifle, clenching his sphincter, smelling his own excitement, and trying to swallow his fear.

I raised my rifle as slowly as I could and took careful aim, remembering to let my breath out halfway and hold it before squeezing the trigger slowly. Oh so slowly.

I shot him. To be precise, I gut-shot him. The four of us tracked him for two hours, following rust-colored drops of blood littering dead leaves and scattered snow, until we found the young buck where he had finally collapsed in the brush, his lungs heaving. He knew he was done for, and so did I. I knew the kindest thing to do was to end his agony quickly with a fast shot to the head. I held the muzzle a few inches from his ear, closed my eyes, and pulled the trigger. When I opened my eyes, I saw that I'd blown *his* nearly out of his head. I staggered back and fell to my knees in the underbrush, where I tried to be sick but couldn't. I just knelt there, turned away from the carnage, while my father finished the job, quickly gutting the deer and slitting his throat. Together, we tied a short rope around the buck's hind legs and hung my "kill" from a tree limb until he stopped dripping. An hour later I started to drag my first buck back to camp, a long ways away. I refused all offers of assistance from dad, Uncle Leland, and cousin Joe. I had caused my buck two hours of agony before killing him, and by God, I would atone by dragging him all the way home.

I hunted for several Novembers after that with my father, uncle and cousins, through high school and on into college. I killed more deer, each of them cleanly shot in the shoulder or neck, each quickly dead. I never choked. I never experienced "buck fever." Dad became proud of my prowess as a shooter, as well as a tracker. He rarely said anything to my face, but I would hear him talking about me with Uncle Leland and their buddies back home, liking what I heard.

Eventually I weaned myself away from hunting, without ever explaining myself. I just came up with excuses—studying for mid-terms, too busy, not feeling well—whatever excuse worked at the time. Finally, Dad stopped asking. I'm sure he thought I didn't have the heart for it anymore, or that I didn't enjoy his company, or that college had raised my consciousness enough that I could no longer stand to kill things.

I never confided to him the real reason I quit hunting, that I quit not because I didn't enjoy the killing but because I was afraid I was enjoying it too much. I know that enjoying the hunt is not unusual. Most hunters enjoy hunting. Ask hunters why they hunt—not the weekend drunks sitting in bars near the woods with their $500 rifles and scopes propped between their legs—but *real* hunters, ask *them* why they hunt, and you'll get some variation of the universal answer: it's the hunting itself, the primal quest for food on the hoof, paw, or wing, the joy of tramping through lightly trammeled woods without getting lost, the relief of escaping the constrictions of the workaday world for a precious few days of freedom in the wild.

To be sure, that was part of the joy for me too. I did like the trekking and the tracking, and I loved pitting my intellect and skills against another animal's instinctive wiliness. But the real lure, the emotional addiction, was the heady feeling each time a deer's head or neck was centered on the cross-hairs of the Weaver two-and-a-half power scope on my Marlin 30-30. I enjoyed thinking about pulling the trigger, enjoyed feeling the trigger release, enjoyed watching the deer drop in his tracks, enjoyed knowing I'd killed him. Every time I killed one, I enjoyed it a little more, and each time I looked forward to killing the next one with even more anticipation. Too much so, I finally realized, sensing the path I was choosing wasn't the path diverging in a snowy wood that would make all difference—at least not the kind of difference I wanted. So I quit, cold turkey.

Two years later I went into the Air Force; two years after that, I was in Vietnam, Laos, Thailand, and Cambodia. I'll not describe the things I saw done there or the things I did myself in those lovely, ugly countries. From today's vantage point, I can convince myself it was just a continuation of my delayed rite of passage, something I had to do to prove something to myself and to my cohorts. Maybe to my father too, a Marine in an earlier Pacific war whose final duty was patrolling the radioactive ruins of Nagasaki after the Japanese surrendered. Dad would have understood what I was saying: that I was telling myself that I was passing into manliness. Yeah I could have said that, and I did, but only to myself. I made a damned good case of it too, even if I never dared meet my own eyes in a mirror while I did.

Now Rick was undergoing a similar transition to manhood, at a similar point in his life. But with Rick, the difference is that his fascination centered on the weapons themselves, weapons of all types: knives, guns, swords, explosives. His interest is genuine. He reads everything he can find about them and is fascinated by their role in warfare and their essential role in American history, if not all history. He's convinced an armed citizenry provides a bulwark a republic's democratic government would ne'er dare breach.

Rick knows, and I know too, that his interest in weaponry also is a way of defining his identity as wholly his own, not his dad's. He's seeking a self that is authentically *him*. His motivation is healthy, a whole lot healthier than mine was, I suspect. I was a mixed-up boy-man for a very long time. And I'm still struggling. But that is another story, several of them, actually. Sometime, I'll be able to tell them. But not now. Oh God no. Not now.

But I was talking about Rick and his attitude toward guns. He knows their history and their use and their place in the world. He favors weapons education as a way of promoting a responsible class of armed citizens. I favor banning guns—all guns, everywhere. In the heat of an argument, I'm apt to propose banning anything that goes boom, from cap pistols to H-bombs, the forced reeducation of hunters and soldiers toward more worthy recreational pursuits, and the certain castration of criminals caught with guns to eradicate testosterone-induced evil from the global gene-pool. A nice moderate view, right? The last thing I want in my house is a gun or any lethal weapon. I'm not all that crazy about the steak knives in the cutlery drawer.

Rick and I have compromised for the sake of family peace. I recognize that my views are not especially balanced or sensible, and we do keep two guns in the house, the .22 pump-action rifle Rick had used that afternoon, a gift from Em's father, and a Ruger .22 semi-automatic pistol he particularly prizes, a gift from my father. I've never fired either weapon, but I did take Rick to the Sportsman's Club firing range to enroll him in their weapons safety course. I was told that fathers (or mothers) must enroll and attend alongside their sons (or daughters). Eventually, I suppose I will do that.

My solution, temporary but hopefully sufficient, was to find a gravel pit 50 miles from the island, where I taught Rick the more obvious aspects of firearm safety, like never pointing a gun or a rifle at anything he did not intend to kill. In a selfless swallowing of my prejudices, I'd even invited my father out to take Rick hunting this fall, and he accepted, eagerly. It wasn't a purely magnanimous act on my part. Secretly, I hoped that Rick would find the reality of hunting—or as in my case, the *thrill* of killing—repulsive. I hoped the bloody results would stick in his craw sooner than they had in mine.

So there you have it, my feelings about guns and Rick's too. To be more precise, our feelings about guns at that particular moment, as we celebrated what felt like my bright future as a published writer, as we had yet another talk about how, with respect to weapons, we would continue to seek a middle ground we both could occupy in good conscience. A sort of permanent demilitarized zone.

But nothing is ever permanent, is it? And demilitarization lasts only until a weapon is cocked and pointed at you.

5

Dan Crawford's call at six a.m. sounded like a summons from God. I had turned on the phone answering machine the day before, with the volume set high so I could monitor it from the deck. The machine bellowed Dan's voice as I emerged from the bedroom.

"It is imperative we talk," he said. "I'll call you back at seven and hourly thereafter until I reach you." He hung up just as I reached for the phone.

I wondered how I could call him back, rather than waiting for his return call in an hour. I dialed *-6-9, but got only a recording that the originating caller's number was blocked. I didn't have caller ID, so I had no clue where he was calling from, but probably he hadn't called from his old office at Boeing, and it was even less likely he had called from home. Jane would have called if Dan had returned home. I tried his old office number anyway. No answer, not even a recording; no voice mail or phone machines at Boeing Legal, apparently.

There was little to do except wait until seven o'clock. I ate some cereal, shaved, dressed, and read the entire newspaper, except the classifieds. And lo, it became seven o'clock.

At 7:15, I replayed Dan's message, just to be sure. He must have been detained. I would wait until eight, but no longer. If he didn't call then, I would do something, call Jane perhaps, which I certainly didn't feel like doing. I have to admit to some worry at that point. You could count on Dan's punctuality; he was fanatical about being on time. Twice, we'd ridden to work together. Both times he chewed me out for picking him up two minutes late. If Dan Crawford said he would be

31

somewhere at a certain time, a yuppie could set his Swiss chronometer by it.

I awakened Rick and Miguel, offering to take them out for breakfast if they would be up and ready to go at 8:15. "One hour, guys," I said. And left, returning to the living room and the classified ads to wait for Dan's call. But I knew that he wouldn't call at eight, either, and that I would have to call Jane.

A few minutes past eight, she verified she hadn't heard from Dan, either. I tried to consider my options as I drove to Poulsbo with the boys, but quickly got distracted. We had decided on Farley's Family Restaurant. The boys would enjoy Farley's; I wouldn't. I had this grudge, you see. I had bounced a check there, about a year ago. It wasn't a big check; I still remember the amount: $13.78. When my bank said my check had bounced, I went to the restaurant immediately with $13.78 in cash, to redeem my bad check and restore my good name. That would be fine, the manager said, but he also insisted on a $15 service fee.

"Nonsense," I said. "I shouldn't have to pay a penalty that is more than the amount of the check, especially since it was an innocent accident." I did a rough, exaggerated calculation to fortify my case. "Why, I must spend at least a thousand dollars a year here...."

"And we do appreciate it," the manager said. "But we don't make exceptions." Then he elaborated their policy on bad checks. Which was to turn everything over to the County Sheriff.

"Fine!" I said, fully enraged, the bright red cock's comb atop my head flamingly erect. "We'll just handle it all in court, then!" I knew he would back down.

"Suit yourself," came the infuriatingly calm reply.

"Okay! Fine! I will!"

I huffed out of the restaurant and drove immediately to the Poulsbo Post Office, where I bought a money order for $13.78, wrapped it in a piece of paper on which I scrawled a terrifically persuasive restatement of my case, and mailed it to the restaurant.

Then I put it out of my mind, until a certified letter from the Kitsap County Sheriff arrived a month later. They had assessed a $100 fine and would issue a bench warrant for my arrest in three days unless they received payment in full: the fine, plus the value of the bad check, plus Farley's $15 service fee—a grand total of $128.78. They offered me a choice: I could pay by certified check or money order.

"Unfair!" my ego cried as I bought another postal money order to pay for this latest miscarriage of justice. I vowed to never again darken Farley's Family Restaurant's mock-Nordic decor with my scowling visage, a vow that lasted an entire week. Farley's remains the only consistently dependable purveyor of reasonably priced, consistently palatable food within ten miles of Bainbridge Island. Well, the only one that still treated smokers like customers, anyway.

So now, a year later, I sat in a big plastic-covered booth with Miguel and Rick, watching them inhale tall stacks of hotcakes while I inhaled large amounts of smoke and tried to think about Dan Crawford instead. I finally remembered the restaurant had a pay phone back by the rest rooms, First, I called the two lawyers Dan had mentioned two nights ago; neither lawyer told me anything. "That would be unethical, sir," was the flavor of the their prissy responses when I asked about Dan.

Then I called the mysterious Mr. Smith. Smith wasn't in either, and the woman who answered the phone would not confirm that Smith was a Boeing functionary. She said, "I have no idea why Mr. Smith would have called Mr. Crawford." She offered to have Mr. Smith call me. I told her not to bother.

My last call was to my own phone machine. When it answered, I dialed the device's access code and listened to Dan's six o'clock call again. It said nothing new, and there were no other messages on the tape. I returned to the booth and smoked the last cigarette in the pack.

On the way out, I asked the manager if my money order for $13.78 had ever arrived. He smiled, remembering. It hadn't. In my rage a year ago, I hadn't kept the carbon copy, of course. So I was out that $13.78 as well.

By the time we reached home, my mood was foul. The boys, ever alert, opted to occupy themselves in Rick's room. I put Vivaldi's Four Seasons on the stereo. Vivaldi's passion, controlled, measured, melodic, sometimes improved my mood. Eight movement later, towards the end of "Summer," I felt less homicidal.

It was time to do something about Dan. I called Mommie Dearest again, who still hadn't heard anything, then told the boys of my plans.

"Don't worry about us, dad. We'll hike up to Jiffy Mart and get a couple pizzas if you're not back in time for dinner." Rick sounded relieved.

I parked the Rabbit at the Winslow terminal and walked aboard the 11:15 ferry. By noon, I was in the offices of Holtzman, Hardy, and Horace in the Norton Building, just in time to be informed that everyone was at a partners' luncheon and did I care to make an appointment? I did, for one o'clock.

The same routine at Gatsby, McLain, and McGinty, one floor up, produced a 1:30 appointment. I took the elevator to the lobby and descended the very long escalator through the parking garage to the First Avenue side of the building, my destination the deli in the Colman Building across the street. Whereupon I discovered my resources consisted of a single dollar bill and two nickels, and the deli didn't take credit cards, not even my overheated Visa. Not in the mood to hie myself off in search of an ATM, my lunch consisted of a cup of coffee. Fortunately, I had picked up a fresh pack of Camels from the soggy carton at home, so lunch wasn't completely without nourishment. And there was food for the mind too, an abandoned *Seattle PI* from the day before.

John Hahn's always interesting column chronicled his annual conversion from a hairy visage to a smooth one. His winter beard was gone now, he said, a sign of summer more certain than the Mariners' first sweep of a three-game series with the detested Yankees, winning by a cumulative 18 runs. We Seattleites rejoiced in such anomalies.

An article in the paper's business section about a major new Boeing "Star Wars" contract caught my eye. Dan Crawford's name appeared near the end of the story, which surprised me, since Dan no longer worked for Boeing. Then I realized the article was one of those canned PR pieces designed to reassure Seattleites that all remained well with their home-grown aerospace giant, now headquartered in Chicago. Written months ago, the article was full of ancient news about the many significant government contracts Boeing had received over the last year. Dan Crawford was described as "...negotiator of several contracts, totaling more than three billion dollars in revenue for The Boeing Company."

Obviously, Boeing wanted folks to know that Dan Crawford was a stellar asset, probably being groomed for something big. So why would they have let him go? What had caused his sudden—as yet unreported—fall? Seemed to me that Dan must have done something very wrong or posed a threat to someone very important. Perhaps someone named Smith?

Eventually, one o'clock rolled around. From then until one-twenty, I waited in Holtzman, Hardy, and Horace's tasteful smoky gray and mauve reception area, trying to ignore the acidic residue of the smoky liquid lunch now roiling my gut. As I waited in growing discomfort, I tried to remember what Victor Howard Horace looked like, but came up with no mental picture, until I was ushered into his offices. Then I remember his most salient feature: the number "3." Three given names, three chins, and a mouthwash whose aroma was so overwhelming that he must have drunk three fingers of it.

"I'm afraid we still don't need your services, Mister Eastman."

I was startled to have been remembered. Maybe he had some sort of card system to jog his memory, with my name filed under "Writer, Legal: don't use."

I smiled my most agreeable smile, the same one that hadn't obtained any work last time, and came right to the point.

"I'm not looking for work, just information. I'm here to find out if you know Dan Crawford."

"Can't say that I do."

"That's odd. He mentioned you just the other night. Dan Crawford." I watched for a change in his demeanor. "Used to be with Boeing."

There. All three chins quivered a little.

"Oh, yes. I remember." He consulted a Rolodex file next to his phone. Yep, he kept his memory on two-inch by four-inch cards. "Yes, Mr. Crawford did stop in last week." He looked at me and visibly stiffened. "May I ask the nature of your interest in Mister Crawford?"

"We're friends."

"And?"

"And he told me he had spoken to you about joining your firm."

"Yes."

"What came of that?"

"Oh, well, I'm afraid I'm not at liberty to talk about that. You understand. Lawyer-client and all that."

"Dan is your client?"

"No…not exactly."

"Then you are not bound by lawyer-client confidentiality. Right?" Gotcha.

"That is correct. But I still can divulge nothing of our conversation. The privacy laws, you know. All of us must pay heed to them, even writers." He gave me a smile as big as a large-mouth bass as he spit out the hook. "I'm afraid you will have to ask Mister Crawford yourself. Since you are friends. Now, if you will excuse me, I do have a rather full schedule. Thanks for stopping by."

So I went to keep my appointment with Garfield Gatsby, he of the two family names. Perhaps Garfield Gatsby and Victor Howard Horace could get together and combine their monikers into some normal-sounding names for themselves. It was not a kindly thought.

Gatsby repeated Horace's lecture about propriety and privacy, virtually verbatim. Like Horace, he was polite, even superficially cordial, in an oily sort of way, but left no doubt that I was wasting my time as well as his. Heading back to the ferry terminal, I wondered if Horace had called Gatsby about me. Probably, while I was waiting for the elevator to Gatsby's office.

Both men had been unhelpful and entirely too...What? Disdainful? Sure. Polite? Yeah, superficially. But mostly? Unctuously pompous, dissimilar traits most successfully conjoined by lawyers, CEOs, and politicians.

I had expected their lofty disdain. But it was their practiced slickness that convinced me both lawyers were hiding something. I had been able to confirm that Dan had spoken to both men—and sensed that both men wished he hadn't. All their insincere courtesy, layered with propriety, had one purpose: they wanted to shut me out. But they didn't want to make me mad enough to pursue it any further.

We would see about that. Trouble was, I didn't know what or whom to pursue. I drummed my fingers on a table in the ferry boat cafeteria on my way back to the island, wishing I could figure it out, wishing I had cash for a beer, wishing it wasn't illegal to smoke inside the boat.

A bottle of Henry's finest on the deck at home produced no wisdom either. Rick brought me a second bottle.

"Something wrong, dad?"

I told him, in abbreviated form, about Jane asking me to find out what was happening with Dan, then swore him to secrecy.

"Jesus, dad, I'm sorry. I forgot to tell you. Dan Crawford called while you were gone—about an hour ago. He didn't leave a message but he sounded, I don't know, kinda worried?"

I called Jane immediately, but she hadn't heard from Dan. Her fear was intensifying. So was mine. This was completely atypical behavior for Dan. To call and say he would call back, then not to call. Then to finally call but not leave a message or a number where I could reach him. Where was he? Was he on the run? If so, from whom? And why?

"Anything Miguel and I can do to help?"

I shook my head. I couldn't even think of anything I could do.

"Maybe I could talk to DJ," Rick saw my confusion. "'DJ,'" he continued. "Deej. Dan Junior. Maybe he's got some ideas. Maybe his dad's said something to him."

Sounded good to me. So much for keeping it a secret. Hell, I didn't even know what we were keeping secret.

Rick made the call and reported back immediately.

"He's not at home but he'll call me later."

For the next hour or so, Miguel, Rick and I spit-balled theories about Dan, speculating on the kind of trouble he might be in. All we knew for sure was that Boeing had left him go, that Dan had talked to a couple of evasive lawyers, and that his normal, steady patterns seemed all a-jumble.

Rick and Miguel played the game well, being less inhibited by having experienced fewer instances of their off-the-wall ideas berated as being off the wall.

"He's selling secrets," Rick said. "To the commies."

"He's a hit man for Boeing." Miguel said.

"He was blackmailing someone and got bumped off," I said, joining in the spirit. "Wait a minute, guys, let's look at it this way. Let's say he *has* done something wrong, I don't know what, but something that got him into big trouble. Embezzlement, maybe. Let's say he's into Boeing for big bucks. What would he do if he thought he was in danger?"

"He would go to the cops?" Miguel offered.

"No, dufus," Rick said. "They'd lock him up. He would hide out somewhere. That's why he doesn't leave a phone number. He probably thinks our phone is tapped."

"Yeah! He's probably setting up a new identity and is going to disappear until this thing blows over."

"Okay, okay," I said. "Let's run with that. Say he's trying to disappear. Where would he go?"

Rick remembered. "DJ said one time that they've got this place out in the Olympics somewhere, by Port Angeles, I think. Some kind of cabin in the woods. Maybe there?"

"Do you know where it is?"

"No, but DJ does. He's talked about it enough. It's way the hell out in the sticks. No phone, no electricity, nothing. He calls it their survival place if the big one comes." Rick looked like he wanted to say more, like, "*shouldn't we have a place like that?*"

"Hey, that sounds promising to me. The hideout, I mean, not the big one."

I called Jane and she said the cabin was out past Port Angeles, "Up in the hills somewhere." She'd never been there, she said, but Dan took the boys there two or three times a year, using the cabin as a base for hiking the Olympics.

So we went over to the Crawfords' to wait for DJ, after throwing some old clothes and hiking boots into the hatchback trunk of the VW, "the "Cwazy Wabbit," as Rick called it. I didn't know it at the time, but Rick also managed to slip his pump-action .22 under the clothing.

Dan Junior returned home around seven and we all headed toward Port Angeles. It was nearly eight o'clock when we crossed the Hood Canal Bridge and stopped at a picnic area to eat the ham sandwiches Mommie Dearest had sent with us. She had opted not to come along, preferring to stay hear the phone in case Dan Senior called.

It was almost ten o'clock by the time we reached Port Angeles, and by ten-thirty we were lost in the mountains, a couple thousand feet above the Strait of Juan de Fuca. We weren't terribly lost. I mean, I knew where we were, and I knew where Port Angeles was—down there, somewhere, towards the water. But we hadn't been able to find the turnoff to the Crawford cabin.

"Well, DJ," I said, trying to be magnanimous. "Things look different in the dark."

At that moment, the Cwazy Wabbit ran out of gas. I turned off the headlights to conserve the battery as we coasted to a stop by the side of the road. There wasn't another vehicle in sight. I stepped out of the car to listen. The night air carried the sound of no other vehicles, just the metallic pinging of the VW's cooling engine.

Pushing and shoving, Miguel, DJ, and I got the car turned around and headed back toward Port Angeles. Rick steered the car. Then our work began, for we had to push the Rabbit up a long incline before we could coast down the other side. Fortunately, the grade wasn't steep, just interminable. After awhile, I stopped thinking about how far we had to go and concentrated on keeping a steady pace that my lungs and legs could tolerate. Rick offered to trade places with me, but I declined; it would be impossible to regain momentum if we stopped, even momentarily. Finally, we reached the crest of the hill, the highest point for miles around, and I crawled back behind the wheel. With luck, we could coast all the way to a gas station in Port Angeles. Maybe by then my lungs, legs, and shoulders would stop spasming.

We made it in one long, roller-coaster ride. I want to testify to the terrors of piloting a dead car for 26 miles at high speed in the dark, without headlights and, after three applications, without power assist on the brakes. And I also want to testify to the wonders of Volkswagen handling; even ancient Cwazy Wabbits have *Fahrvergnugen*. We met one car on the way, and I'm sure he was startled as his headlights picked up a silver streak hurtling by in the dark. My right leg trembled with the effort of maintaining more or less constant pressure on the brake pedal. When we finally stopped, I felt like the last-place finisher of a marathon for one-legged people.

Our momentum ebbed a few feet short of the gas pumps in an "all night" Arco station. It was an Arco station, all right. But it sure wasn't open all night. We debated whether or not to leave the Cwippled Wabbit there. For me, there was little choice. I had barely enough strength to limp across the street to the Hotel Juan de Fuca. We left a note under the windshield wiper of the car, saying we would reclaim the car in the morning. Wouldn't want the dumb bunny towed away.

Hotel Juan de Fuca had one room vacant, the bridal suite. One hundred and forty dollars, please, plus tax. I looked at the three twenties in my wallet, and stepped out on the stoop to consider options. Sleep in the car? Hike on to another, cheaper motel? My legs twitched in agony.

Miguel handed me his silver-colored American Express card. His name was embossed on it, black on no-credit-limit silver: MIGUEL SHARP.

"Thank you, Mister Sharp," the desk clerk said to me after signing us in to the suite. His manner was deferential in the extreme, to Miguel's amusement. Then the desk clerk ushered us into the most outrageous motel room in the world. A round bed ten feet in diameter dominated one side of the room, almost lewd in its red velvet upholstery, tufted into billowy puffs that looked like huge fuzzy Maraschino cherries. Apt symbology. The walls were covered with red wallpaper. Draperies of crimson velvet, closed for privacy, matched the bed's headboard. Had they had ever been open? The suite's intended tenants would care little for scenery. Across the room from the bed was a small bar, clad in red vinyl, topped with—what else?—red laminate. Soft drinks and mixes filled the tiny refrigerator under the bar. Airline-sized bottles of booze filled a basket on the bar. A few feet from the bar was a carmine-colored, heart-shaped bathtub for two. Aeration jets ran across its bottom. The adjacent bathroom was done in gory red tile, trimmed with black. No bidet, I noted; this was, after all, the Olympic Peninsula, not Seattle's Olympic Four Seasons Hotel. A large-screen projection television faced the bed and could be viewed, upside-down, if desired, through the mirror on the ceiling above the bed. The mirror was the same diameter as the bed.

"It's a Norman Bates wet dream," I said. "See what you guys have to look forward to when it's your time?"

Rick vowed to remember this place. Our laughter followed the desk clerk out the door. Eventually, the boys recovered long enough to turn on the water and fill the big tub with water, which soon burbled as merrily as they did, stripping down to cannon-ball into the tub. I found a James Bond videotape and plugged it in to the VCR, then swiveled the big TV towards the tub. An underwater fandango between Bond and a suggestively named, lasciviously lusty heroine/villainess was the first scene in the movie.

At the boys' request, I ordered a giant pizza from the handy bed-side menu, charging it to Mister Sharp.

Then it was time for me to excuse myself and leave the boys the run of the place. Miguel's money had paid the night's rent on the pleasure dome, after all. And hey, I was fifteen once.

I don't remember the name of the all-night restaurant I found on the main drag. It looked like a Denny's and it smelled like a Denny's, and the food was nearly as edible as a Denny's. I spent my time trying to take stock of what I knew about this whole situation. I didn't know much. I suspected our search for Dan Crawford's cabin in the woods would turn out to be another wild goose chase, like my visit to the lawyers' offices. In all likelihood, we would know nothing more after finding the cabin, assuming we could find the cabin. I suppose there was a slim chance that we would find Dan holed up there. But I doubted it.

Eventually, I remembered the financial records Jane had given me. If I had them now, I could check them over, maybe find some clue, perhaps a check stub made out to someone I recognized, or maybe to a travel agent or an airline. But I didn't have the records with me, and I couldn't remember where I'd left them. Probably on the kitchen counter at home, where most things ended up in our house.

I must have sat there for a couple hours or more, drinking coffee, making notes, trying to puzzle things out. I was beginning to feel a lot like Inspector Clouseau, except I *knew* I was dumb.

Dumb to be up all night, too, I gave it up and walked back to the motel. This time I didn't limp. Mega-doses of caffeine and nicotine can cure anything, although the Surgeon General adamantly refuses to admit it.

The boys were asleep on the big bed, radially arranged, their heads at the perimeter, their feet at the center. The roll-away cot promised by the clerk was set up at poolside, its coverlet carefully turned down. The coverlet was as red as the sheets, consistency being the hallmark of witless design.

Out of curiosity, I opened the drapes. Right. There was no window at all, just more red flocked wallpaper behind the drapery.

6

Breakfast was my treat, back at my midnight cafe. I chose the continental breakfast, a cinnamon roll nuked *ala* Chernobyl, with a big glass of orange juice to cool the molten core.

On the way to the cafe, I had filled up with gas and picked up a free tourist map, courtesy of Arco of Port Angeles, home of the famous closed-at-dusk-all-night-long station. DJ scoured the map and spotted the road leading to their cabin almost immediately. We had run out of gas just a half-mile short of the turnoff to the cabin.

By nine-thirty, we were at the cabin, looking at a door secured with a nuclear attack-proof padlock. Since the padlock was in place and locked, it was safe to assume Dan wasn't lurking inside. The key to the padlock was hidden over the door, in a short length of rain gutter protecting the entry, not the most original place to hide a key to a bunker. DJ unlocked the padlock, opened the door and restored the key to the gutter.

Built of rock and peeled Douglas-fir logs, the cabin's interior dimensions were about sixteen feet by twenty. A fireplace of river rock with a slate hearth spanned one narrow end of the cabin. Opposite was the kitchen, complete with a old hand pump at an equally ancient and well-preserved porcelain-on-cast-iron sink with drain-boards, set into a bank of cabinets spanning the wall. The place would have made a decent set for a movie produced with Utah money, something with a title like "Up From the Ashes Freedom Family," its plot and casting predictable: mom, dad, two kids (young boy, girl in early but promising pubescence), cute mongrel named "Dog." Post-holocaust life in the wild, coping with Mother Nature's unending malice: blizzards, avalanches, near-starvation, beasts of long tooth and bloody claw, absence of intellectual stimulation. All the things that make families strong and child abuse such a national disgrace.

The kitchen appeared to be stocked to outlast most foreseeable fallout patterns. Foot-deep shelves flanked the small window over the sink, continuing around both long walls for six or seven feet. Canned and freeze-dried food filled the shelves. The circular pot rack above a free-standing propane-fueled stove held an iron skillet, stainless steel pans, a blue spatter-ware colander. All the comforts of home, with enough food for a Latter Day Saint's basement. Quantities that had never graced an Eastman pantry.

Rick took note of the heavy interior wooden shutters lined with lead, designed to close securely across the cabin's three windows. DJ explained that similar half-inch sheets of lead were sandwiched between the logs and the cabin's vertical fir board and batten interior paneling. Overhead, the same shielding gleamed dully between the rafters. Uncharitably, I wondered what sense it made to survive a nuclear blast and weeks of fallout only to succumb to lead poisoning.

The place slept eight, DJ proclaimed, two in a double bed in the small downstairs bedroom, six on padded cots in the loft. I noticed that a gun case built into the rocks to the left of the fireplace held weapons and backup weapons for all residents. Enough ammunition to weather several sieges by local refugees lined the shelves beneath the guns and rifles, shiny ranks of tiny bald soldiers. Reinforcements in boxed ranks queued up in rear echelons, ready to be summoned to the front.

I checked the kitchen for signs of recent habitation. A couple of strokes on the hand pump sent a gush of water into the sink.

"Two-thousand-gallon tank under the floor," said DJ.

"All right!" said Rick and Miguel in unison.

The pine table in the kitchen was almost bare. A stack of typing paper formed a neat pile at one side, sharpened pencils carefully aligned alongside. I picked up the top sheet from the stack and held it slantwise to the sunlight streaming through the kitchen window. Then put it back on the stack. Sherlock Holmes would have found indentations from a previous missive and filled them with pencil lead shavings, or soot, or snot, or something. I detected pristine paper.

Nonetheless, before I could stop myself, I lowered my head to table top height and sighted across the surface of the table, looking for pencil tracks in the wood itself. The boys eyed me curiously. I could have pretended to be looking for a contact lens, if I had thought more quickly. If I wore them.

DJ said they rarely used the cabin any more. They used to come more often when he and his siblings were younger, but they hadn't been there since last summer. "We restocked the pantry then."

I looked more closely at the cans and packages on the pantry shelves to see if there were any gaps that would indicate any food consumed recently. No obvious clues there, either. It looked like their visit last year was the last time anyone had been in the cabin.

I asked him, "Notice anything out of place? Anything different from last time?" I nodded toward the gun rack. "Guns all there?"

He looked. "Hey! I think one of the automatics is missing. A Walther PPK."

"Like James Bond's!" Miguel said.

"Yeah!" echoed Rick.

"Any others missing?" I said.

"I don't think so. We had only two PPKs. I think both of them were here last time. I can't be sure. I suppose one could be at home."

"We'll check when we get back," I said. "Wow, DJ, I didn't know your dad was such a...whaddayacallit?"

"Survivalist," Rick supplied.

Dan said, "Well, he doesn't talk much about that kind of stuff. He doesn't want a lot of people knowing about this place, you know?"

I did. It would be hard to have to shoot friends to keep them out of your shelter. Except now that I knew where they kept the key, I could always make myself a copy, anytime before the "big one." Sufficiently motivated, I could probably get Em and Rick and me here first.

The tiny cubbyhole of a bedroom on the first floor revealed no secrets. The bed looked like it could have been slept in recently. But how would I know? Does an unmade bed look any more unmade a year later?

The boys crowded in behind me.

"The bed was made up when we left last year. We always put on fresh sheets so the beds will be ready to use, you know?"

Aha! I *had* found a clue. Two clues, if you count the possibly missing gun. Someone *had* been sleeping in Dan's bed. I felt like Papa Bear as I climbed the steep ladder to the loft, half expecting to find a young blonde asleep on a cot sized just right for her. Instead I found rolled-up sleeping bags neatly stowed at the foot of each cot. I wondered what I would have done if I had actually found someone up there. WWPBD? What would Papa Bear do?

Ah, yes. He'd look for paw prints. I headed outside. The boys followed.

"Would you recognize the pattern from the tires on your dad's car, DJ?"

"Big mud and snows on the Cherokee. They've got great big lugs on 'em, in a funny pattern, more rows on the outside than the inside. I know because dad bought them in Port Angeles last summer, and I watched them being put on. And the Cherokee isn't home, so dad must have it!"

The boys immediately began crawling around on their hands and knees, all around the front of the cabin. Miguel found the tracks first.

"C'mere, DJ! Are these them?"

They were, in DJ's estimation. I agreed. They had an asymmetric design, a solid rib down the center, with three interlocking rows of big lugs on the outside, two on the inside.

"They look fresh to me," I said. "Made since the last rain, anyway."

Rick said, "Let's check with the weather service and find out when it rained last."

"Right," I said, reaching up and ruffling his hair. I used to do that all the time; I used to reach down to do it. I consoled myself with the thought that it looked like Rick had already achieved one of my two major goals as an adolescent—six feet of height. When had that happened? He could probably do one-handed pushups too. I was pretty sure he'd probably already achieved my other major adolescent goal as well. I'd just as soon not ask.

"Okay, guys," I said, moving back into the cabin. I pulled a piece of paper off the stack on the table and started making notes. "It looks like Dan was here all right. At least Dan's tires were here. And the revolver is missing."

"Not a revolver, dad. It's an automatic."

"Right. A Walker PKK."

"Wal*ther* PPK, dad."

"Right. Walther PPK. Anyway, it looks like Dan was here. Probably recently, judging by the freshness of the tire tracks. Maybe even last night."

Miguel interjected, "Then he's probably still around!" We all looked at him for elaboration. "Well, it figures, doesn't it? If he was here last night, he must still be in the area, or we would have met the Cherokee when we drove out here this morning."

"Go on," I said.

"Well, I mean, why would he leave the area? Nobody knows he's here. Hardly anyone knows about this place, so he'd hole up here, wouldn't he? I would. It's got everything you need."

DJ agreed. "He'll probably be back again pretty soon! Bet he's just out getting some beer or something."

"Yeah," Rick said. "We better wait around for him."

That made some sense. But if Dan had been here the night before last, instead of last night, he could have already driven back to Seattle, or even taken the ferry from Port Angeles across the Strait to Vancouver Island. For that matter, he could be anywhere by now.

Something didn't feel right. That little voice was there again, trying to tell me something. But what? It certainly felt like we were close. Dan might still be around, perhaps nearby. I wondered if he had driven into Port Angeles yesterday to place his calls to me.

Suddenly I remembered Dan Senior's financial records. There had to be some reason they kept popping into my mind. Some clue, maybe a check, or a note. That must have been what that little voice was trying to tell me.

"Tell you what, guys. I have some of Dan's bank records that might tell us something, but I left them at home. Maybe I should drive back to the island and pick them up. Would you guys be all right here, if I left you to wait for Dan, in case he shows up?" Their eyes got big. They nodded enthusiastically.

"If I leave now, I can be back in a couple hours. If Dan gets back before I do, tell him he owes us all a big steak dinner. And a good explanation. How does that sound?"

Sounded pretty good to them, even if it sounded pretty weak to me. But what else could we do? Leave a note on the cabin door? There had to be some reason why those bank records kept coming to mind, some reason they were important, and I've learned to trust my hunches. It didn't feel right to leave three 15-year-olds in the woods alone. On the other hand, they were fifteen years old, not ten, or five—and there were three of them. They certainly could take care of themselves, and the cabin was stocked with everything a teenaged boy might want.

And then some. I had to handle one more detail before I could leave them in good conscience. I called Rick to my side and rested my arm on his shoulder. I addressed all three boys.

"Now, you guys are going to be here alone. So you have to promise me you won't do anything dangerous and that you'll stay right here at the cabin and not wander off." They nodded their understanding. "I'm leaving Rick in charge." I felt him stand a little straighter.

"And I don't want any of you touching any of those guns in the case." Rick went stiff at what probably felt like an unnecessary admonition. I squeezed his shoulder and he seemed to relax a bit.

"So promise this old pacifist, okay? No guns. And no shooting. All right?"

"Sure, dad," Rick said. "Don't worry. I'll take good care of things." DJ and Miguel nodded. "We'll be careful," Rick added.

"I know you will, guys. I know I can count on all of you."

Twenty minutes later, I rolled past the "all-night" Arco and the hotel, and turned onto Highway 101 toward home. Cresting a hill fifteen minutes later, I was dazzled by sunlight and flipped down the sun visor. A bundle of papers dropped in my lap. I grabbed one piece while the others slid to the floor. It was a bank statement for the joint checking account of Daniel and Jane Crawford.

As I turned around and sped back to Port Angeles and up the hills to the cabin, I had a deeply sick feeling in the pit of my stomach, like I do whenever I've done something particularly stupid that's going to hurt someone.

When I got to the cabin and called out for them, the silence was deafening. The boys were gone.

"Heart in your throat" doesn't begin to describe my escalating panic as I searched the cabin quickly, then forced myself to check more methodically. Draped across the foot of the bed downstairs was a jacket—DJ's, I think. I couldn't imagine that he would have gone outside without it, given the chill in the air. The boys weren't supposed to be away from the cabin, anyway. Maybe they had left a note. I looked everywhere but couldn't find one.

Dammit. There had to be something. Please, God, *something*. But I found nothing and, except for Dan Junior's jacket, could detect no signs of a hasty departure or a struggle.

Until something caught my eye at the doorway. I knelt to look more closely.

Four parallel scratches were gouged deeply across the left side of the wooden door jamb. Reddish-brown streaks lined each furrow. Streaks that had to be blood.

Tears clouded my eyes. I knew immediately that Rick had made those gouges in the wood. Of the three boys, he was the only lefty, and he would have reached for the doorway with his left hand while being dragged out.

Oh, God, Rick. What have they done with you? My fingertips throbbed in sympathy with Rick's pain as his fingernails tore into the wood.

I ran to the car. Then got out and locked the cabin door and replaced the key in the gutter. At least I could protect whatever clues had been left behind. At least I could lock the barn door after the ponies had been rustled.

I drove as fast as the Rabbit's arthritic joints and galumphing heart could carry me. When my right hand wasn't rowing the shift lever, it was triggering the horn. I don't know why it was doing that. Maybe it was trying to be a siren. Maybe if my right hand hadn't been thus occupied, it would have reached up and strangled me for being such a derelict father. Christ, what a piece of shit I was. First my wife leaves me, knowing I'll never make anything of myself, then my son and his two best friends are stolen away because of my stupidity. Some husband. Some father. Someone needed to put me out of my misery.

I forced myself to try to think. Who could have done this? And why? It had to be related to Dan Crawford. Too few people knew of our trip to the cabin for the boys' kidnapping to have been planned in advance. It had to have been opportunistic, which meant that someone must have been shadowing us. I wanted to believe a kinder, gentler explanation, that Dan had returned to the cabin, gathered up the boys and taken them into town for lunch. Sure, just like George H. W. Bush's new world order had produced universal peace, love, and tolerance.

Like Rick hadn't been dragged away, kicking and screaming, leaving bloody furrows in the doorway on his way out.

No, the truth was clear. As clear as if Rick had left a note on the table, for he *had* left a message—a bloody, mute cry for help.

The Port Angeles police station is near the court house, on the east side of the town's main drag, Lincoln Street. A crisply dressed cop with three chevrons on his sleeve met me at the door, probably alerted by the arriving squeal of what little tread remained on the Rabbit's tires.

The cop walked me toward his desk, listening carefully to my story. I thought I was amazingly calm, considering.

The cop put up his hand as I paused for breath and said, "Wait a minute, sir." He picked up the phone.

I exhaled in relief, knowing he would be summoning the troops for an all-out search. But listening to his side of the conversation, I finally realized he was talking to someone in the U.S. Park Service, and that they were arguing who had jurisdiction—the Port Angeles Police Department, the Clallam County Sheriff, the Highway Patrol, or the Park Service.

"Well, I dunno," he was saying. "The cabin's on Park Service land. That makes it yours, don't it?"

I slapped the phone out of his hand. "You fucking cocksucker!"

Sarge picked the phone off the floor and looked at it, then looked at me like I was something stuck to the sole of his shoe. "This is a Park Service case if it happened in the park," he said.

I tried to keep my voice down. I failed. "This may be a case of you needing to remove your head from your asshole, you jerkoff!"

Sarge's face reddened as he stood as tall as he could—about five and a half feet on tippy-toes. He started toward me, intending to demonstrate the efficacy of the strangle-hold in restoring order to the police station.

An even shorter officer in even crisper khakis burst through a door from the back of the station. The dual bars on his collar announced his rank. His voice announced his displeasure.

"What in the hell is going on here?"

"Your man here…" I looked at Sarge's nametag for the first time. "Your man Mink is jerking me around, Captain. I've just reported a kidnapping, a triple-fucking kidnapping, but he can't be bothered. He's too busy passing the buck to the Park Service."

"Okay, Mink, take it from the top. What's the deal?" Then he looked at me. "And you keep your mouth shut."

"Go fuck yourself, Captain. I'll shut up when you get off your fat ass and do your job. My boys are gone. They've been kidnapped. What about that is too hard for you to understand? What does it take to get you guys to do something? My boys could still be around, they might even be right here in town, certainly still in the area. And Mink here is talking to the Park Service. Jesus. Who else do you need to get permission from? Want me to call your wife?"

49

The captain looked ready to pounce. Instead he pointed me to a chair. "Sit. Now." His voice barely contained his fury. "Sit right there, right now, and tell me exactly what happened. Then we'll see what we can do."

I took a deep breath and spelled out what I knew, including how I knew the boys had been kidnapped. He didn't interrupt. He took notes as I talked. I told him everything: my name, the boys' names, all about Mommie Dearest and Dan Senior and Dan Senior's disappearance. I told him about Dan's two calls to me yesterday morning.

"What did he say?"

I picked up the phone, dialed my number, and when the answering machine answered, dialed in my code and handed the phone to the captain. "Here," I said. "You can listen to his message yourself."

He sat on the edge of the desk and listened intently, his face a mask of concentration. He made a few more notes on his pad. When he stopped writing, I assumed the recording had ended, but he listened for a few more moments, then looked up at me.

"Yes. Well, I heard the call from Crawford. But..."

"But what?"

"I thought there might also be a ransom message on your recorder. There wasn't." He stared at me. "We do take this seriously, Mister Eastman."

Then the questioning began in earnest. I went over every detail I could remember. Captain Able—he introduced himself at one point—kept taking notes in some kind of shorthand or speedwriting. Sergeant Mink made some phone calls, keeping his voice down.

Captain Able had just finished his interrogation when a gray-green Ford pickup topped by a red gumball machine rolled to a halt in front of the station's double doors. One of the largest men in the world levered himself out of the cab. He had not an ounce of fat on him, just pure muscle and one hell of a lot of it. A silver hard hat was welded to his head, a U.S. Park Service emblem centered over his name—NORM—just above the narrow visor of the hard hat. He ducked his head and entered the station.

"Mornin', Chief. What's all this 'bout a kidnappin'?"

Captain Able repeated my story for Norm Berenson, U.S. Park Service Ranger. He repeated it nearly verbatim, reading from his notes including everything, editing out my profanity and emotion.

Berenson knew of the cabin. "Crawford place. Right. The 'shelter,' we call it. Enough lead in that place t' sink a battleship and enough armament t' outfit a Persian Gulf task force. Any of them guns missin'?"

"One. A Walter-something-something-K…"

"Walther PPK?"

"Yeah, that one. We noticed it was missing this morning, I mean DJ did—Dan Crawford Junior—one of the boys. When I got back to the cabin and the boys weren't there, I didn't notice anything else out of place or different. Except DJ's jacket was there, and…and…those scratches on the door jamb made by my son's fingernails as they drag…drug…dragged…him out."

Right there I lost it, weeping great hot tears of rage at the kidnappers—but mostly rage at myself. For abandoning my son and his friends. For driving my wife away. For losing everyone who made my miserable life worth living.

In two hours, an investigation team was at the cabin. Another group was operating out of the Winslow police station on Bainbridge Island, with BI cops dispatched to my house and the Crawfords' house.

I had ridden with Chief Able to the cabin. Norm Berenson was organizing a Park Service crew to check vehicles in the park for signs of anything suspicious. He would join us at the cabin later. Sergeant Mink was left to coordinate things in Port Angeles. When we left the station, Mink was on the phone to the FBI office in Seattle.

All the touchable interior surfaces in the cabin and around the doorway were dusted for prints, and a technician took mine for comparison. Deputies scoured the ground for tire and foot prints. They found three sets of sneaker prints, and what looked like a couple different sets of lug-soled boot prints. And prints from my own Top-Siders.

Ranger Berenson noted the tire prints of "Japanese mud n' snows" and followed them down the dirt path to the pavement. He hiked up the road on foot, looking for the tell-tale tread in the dirt roads leading off the main road. A half-hour later he returned, saying he would check all the other roads leading off the main highway. He would keep in touch by radio.

Night had fallen when we got back to Port Angeles. Chief Able bought me dinner at some café. I don't remember the name of the café or what we ate—something with lots of dark salty gravy. Chief Able had a Clallam County Sheriff deputy named Jeff drive me back to the island in my Rabbit. The Chief wouldn't hear of me setting off alone. I didn't want to go home at all, but Able persuaded me that any ransom message would likely come to my home, or to the Crawford residence, not the Port Angeles police station.

Jane Crawford was at my place when Deputy Jeff and I arrived at midnight. Like me, she was scared half to death. We tried to comfort and console each other, without much success. The Bainbridge cop who had spent the day manning my phone said he would be leaving now, that Jeff would be staying the night. The Bainbridge cop promised to be back in the morning. I walked him to his patrol car down in the lot next to the house and asked him if he had been the one to tell Mommie Dearest the news.

"Yeah."

"How'd she take it?"

"About the same as you, I imagine." There was kindness in his voice, and more concern than I've ever heard from a cop. I didn't know his name then and didn't ask for it. I'm sure he had never heard of me before today, either.

"Hey, look," he said. "We'll get this guy—these guys. Count on it. Fuckin' creeps."

"I know what you mean."

"Yeah. Yeah, I imagine you do." He tipped his hat, an obsolete and curiously touching gesture. "I better get going. Try to get some sleep if you can, Mister Eastman. Jeff will stand by your phone tonight."

And he left. I still didn't know his name. I hadn't even thought to look at his nametag.

I must have been suffering from emotional overload, for I found myself disbelieving everything. This couldn't be happening. It was too unreal. There was Mommie Dearest, in my house, with a Sheriff's Deputy named Jeff from Port Angeles, all of us waiting for kidnappers to call my phone. Could it be? Could it really be that Rick and Dan Junior and Miguel had all been taken prisoner? That they had been kidnapped by some creep—correction: creeps?

I remember thinking, hoping, that Em or Dan Senior or someone else would drive up with the boys and yell, "Surprise! Fooled you!" And I'd collapse in relief, then get mad, then it would all be okay.

Yeah. All okay. Then maybe I could forgive myself.

Before I went back to the house, I opened the trunk of the Cwazy Wabbit to retrieve the stuff we'd brought to Port Angeles. I picked up a couple of heavy jackets then saw Rick's .22 pump-action rifle on the floor of the trunk.

Oh, Jesus. There would be no upbeat Hollywood ending to this nightmare. Leaning into the trunk, I gripped its raised lid and waited for the shakes to stop.

Eventually, I closed the trunk, leaving everything in place. I don't know what I would have done with Rick's rifle, had I picked it up.

I. Honestly. Do. Not. Know.

What I did was to climb the stairs to the house and put on a pot of coffee and pretend to be rational. We talked some more, Jane and I, saying brave and kind things neither of us felt. I apologized for abandoning the boys. She apologized for getting me mixed up in whatever was going on with her still-missing husband. We agreed there was little point in fixing blame. We both knew who was at fault—me. But we assured each other that neither of us had any idea anything like this would ever happen. We tried to figure how it all tied in with Dan. We came up with zilch.

Jane decided to spend the night in the guest room. Her older kids were spending the night with friends and a Bainbridge cop was manning her phone. Deputy Jeff said he would bunk on my sofa in the living room, so he could hear the phone if it rang.

I wished Em was home. Chief Able had offered to have the San Juan County Sheriff find her and Alice, tell them everything, and get them home. I had asked him not to. I hoped, desperately hoped, that the boys would be back by morning. If not, I hoped Em would call so I could tell her myself. I couldn't stand the thought of some anonymous cop giving her such bad news. Reluctantly, Chief Able had agreed to wait until morning. If Em hadn't been heard from by then, he would step in. I told myself that, somehow, I would get word to Em and Alice, if I had to charter a plane to the San Juans and buzz every bed and breakfast on all the islands.

It was about 4:00 am when I stopped staring at the grooves in the wood paneling of my bedroom ceiling, stopped watching them fill with blood. I finally closed my eyes and fell into a troubled doze. The ransom call came an hour later.

7

The kidnappers were canny. As soon as the phone was answered, they played a 10-second tinny recording of Rick's voice that ripped my heart in half. Deputy Jeff took the call on our speaker phone-answering machine, punching the record button to preserve their recorded message.

"Dad...This is for real, dad. They've got us and they mean business. They say they will...they will kill us unless you tell them where Dan Crawford is. I told them you didn't know, but...."

And that was it, not even the click of someone hanging up the phone. No instructions on how to get in touch. No ransom demand. Nothing except Rick's voice trying to sound brave. Not a single goddamned clue where the boys might be. No clue where the call was coming from, either. The caller ID unit the police had wired into my phone showed "out of area."

Deputy Jeff called Chief Able in Port Angeles immediately, then the Bainbridge police, then the FBI. For each of them, he played back the awful message. Jane and I felt more helpless with each playback of Rick's truncated voice.

"What the hell can we do, Jeff?" I asked when he was done.

"Stay here. Stay by the phone. They'll call again. The FBI says they'll be able to trace it the next time..."

"They didn't trace this one?"

"They don't have that set up yet. In fact, I don't think they were all that sure this was a kidnapping at all, until now."

"Jesus Christ, Jeff. What were they waiting for?"

"Who knows? Anyway, they seem convinced now."

That was scant consolation. All we could hold onto was the fact of the recording itself. The boys were still alive—at least they were when Rick's voice was recorded. I wouldn't let myself dwell on the fact that the recording could have been made anytime before the call was made and all the boys could be dead by now. I could not dwell on that. I *would* not dwell on that. I would hold tight to the thought that the kidnappers would keep all of them alive, in case we insisted on talking to them before making any deal. Thank God, I had enough presence of mind to not voice my fears to Jane. She had enough fears of her own: a kidnapped son and a missing husband.

So we waited. What else could we do? After a bit, Jeff mentioned that they—the police and the FBI—figured the kidnappers probably would call the Crawford place next, with a message from Dan Junior. To further magnify our terror, presumably.

So he drove Jane home. Shortly after they left, the Bainbridge cop from last night arrived with a guy from the phone company, who installed a second line to the house for outgoing calls, so our original line could be kept clear for another ransom calls. The second phone, black as death, sat alongside the white phone on the breakfast bar. After the phone guy left, I sat on a stool at the bar, drinking coffee and smoking cigarette after cigarette, staring at the white phone, willing it to ring. The black phone rang, nearly knocking me off the stool in surprise.

It was the FBI, a secretary informing me that Special Agent Doorham would be there shortly to take over the investigation. They would coordinate everything.

"Thanks a lot. It's about time the FBI takes this seriously."

But I did feel a little better. The FBI was good at this kind of thing. Everyone who watched TV in the fifties and sixties knew that the FBI always got their man. Efrem Zimbalist always returned kidnapped kids unharmed. Didn't he? Sure, and J. Edgar was a real ladies' man who just happened to like wearing frilly undies.

I moved out on the deck and was staring unseeingly at a beautiful scene of sunlight and ships when the house line rang at eight o'clock. The Bainbridge cop answered it, listened for a moment, then waved me to the phone and turned off the recorder.

"It's your lawyer. Keep it short."

It couldn't be my lawyer. I don't have a lawyer. It was Dan Crawford's lawyer.

"Please don't be alarmed, Mister Eastman, and please don't say anything. This is Garfield Gatsby and I am instructed by the gentleman of whom we recently spoke, to give you a phone number where he may be reached. Do you have a piece of paper?" I found a scrap of paper and slid it around to the side of the phone away from the cop. He took the hint and walked out on the deck. I wrote down the number and slipped the piece of paper in my pocket. Gatsby hung up before I could ask him any questions.

The cop walked back in. "Anything important?"

"No, not really." I hesitated, but not for long. I now had the means to contact Dan Crawford. I probably should have given the cop the phone number. But I wanted to talk to Dan myself first. For the moment, I would keep the phone number a secret.

It wasn't all that hard a choice to make. I had heard Rick's call. Until I knew more, I wasn't going to do anything to jeopardize Rick. Yeah, I would use that reason, flimsy as it was. But I also knew my real reason: I now had the means to do something to rectify my mistake. It was my fault that the boys were in danger. I wanted…no, dammit, I *needed* to do something.

"No," I repeated. "Nothing important. Just my lawyer. I need to run into town and sign some papers. I won't be gone long. I'll pick up some stuff for lunch while I'm out."

I stopped at the pay phone in front of the Jiffy Mart in Rolling Bay, dug the scrap of paper out of my pocket and dialed the number, a local island number. Dan answered on the first ring.

"Dan! They've kidnapped Rick and Dan Junior and Miguel— Rick's friend—and they say they will kill them unless I tell them where you are."

"I was afraid of that. I thought I had more time. Wait a minute, let me think. There's got to be a way…."

"What?! Wait?! What's going on, Dan? Did you hear me? I said the boys had been kidnapped! They've got our boys!"

"Calm down, Andy. This is no time to panic."

"Oh, yeah. Right. Tomorrow's the time to panic. Or maybe I should wait until they send me Rick's ear. What's going on, Dan? Just what the bloody hell is going on?"

"I'll explain it all to you, Andy, I promise. Look, it's too compli-cated to explain over the phone. We have to meet somewhere…." You could almost hear the wheels turning. *You* could. I was too upset to hear anything beyond the pounding of my own heart. I was too mad at

Dan and his amazing and completely inappropriate calmness to do any-thing except breathe rapidly. Finally Dan spoke, naming a place not far from where I was calling. A place on the island. He would be there at ten o'clock. So would I, by God. So would I. I looked at my watch. An hour and forty minutes from now.

"Andy," he said, "don't let anyone follow you. That's imperative. We can't involve the police or the FBI in this."

"Why not?"

"Just do as I say, Andy, or forget about meeting me."

"You mean you would sacrifice your son, and mine, and Miguel, just to keep your secrecy?"

"I have no choice. You don't either, Andy. I'm sorry, but that's the way it is. You'll understand when we meet."

There was little more to say, except one thing he had to know.

"I swear to God, Dan, if anything happens to Rick because you got me into this—whatever *this* is—I will kill you with my own two hands, you sorry son of a bitch."

"I understand. I'm truly sorry, Andy."

I hung up and stood there for a moment, hanging onto the phone receiver. Then I got back into the car and started it up. Then shut it off and went into the Jiffy Mart, bought some bread and peanut butter and a couple packs of cigarettes, and went home.

I wasn't home when the second recorded call from Rick came in. Instead, I was talking to Dan in a dank corner of an old fruit and vege-table stand that had been abandoned since 1942, when the island's Japanese population was relocated to retention camps after Pearl Har-bor. Had I known of the second ransom call at the time, I would have treated Dan with even less humanity than our country treated its Japa-nese citizens. But I didn't know about the call; Instead, I was trying to get information from Dan, the only way I knew how, by not saying much. I swear, it was the hardest thing I've ever done, keeping my mouth closed when I wanted to open it really wide and bite his head off.

"You're sure no one followed you here?" he asked. I shook my head.

"No, no, I suppose you were careful." I kept my mouth closed. I stared at him, wondering when he would say something meaningful. Finally he did.

"You know much about Star Wars?" I nodded. Who didn't? The Strategic Defense Initiative, Reagan's post-menopausal wet-dream, had morphed into an equally costly but more doable limited missile shield under Bush I, Clinton, and Bush II. The Boeing Company's profits had soared as a result.

"I got Boeing all of our Star Wars contracts, Andy. Every one of them, all by myself. Those babies are mine, three billion dollars' worth." I nodded for him to continue. I should care about Star Wars?

"I got them by blackmail."

Whoa. I'm pretty sure my eyebrows shot upward as Dan continued.

"Look, I have to give you a little background, so you'll understand, okay?" I leaned back against a Coca Cola sign that had been new in 1940, lighted another Camel, and listened as he finished his tale.

By the time he was done, I had smoked the rest of my pack and started another, and didn't know what to think. Dan's story was implausible on its surface, but I was prepared to give him the benefit of considerable doubt. Kidnappers *had* taken our boys, after all, which added credence to his conspiracy theory, and I couldn't imagine why Dan would concoct a fairy tale just to explain away a kidnapping. But I also wasn't all that sure he was in his right mind. For that matter, I wasn't sure I was.

Dan sounded rational, but I know that state fairly well. Sounding rational, I mean. I sound that way, too, especially just before I step off into the void. For me, that happens toward the end of marital arguments of serious merit, usually just after Em has made an unassailable point and I'm about to go ballistic in a way that not even Star Wars could neutralize.

"Mommie Dearest must know none of this, Andy. I'm sure you can see that."

Indeed. If Dan told Jane what he'd told me, she would be in great jeopardy; she too would become a target of the conspirators. So would I, for that matter—so *was* I, because now I *did* know what Dan knew. But was it the truth? His tale of corporate corruption and governmental greed made allegations of aerospace company payoffs in the late sixties and early seventies look like donations to a church auction. Moreover, if Dan's story was accurate, those involved in the conspiracy would not quibble over a few dead bodies. Not Dan's, not Jane's, not mine. Certainly not our boys'.

According to Dan, there was hardly a high-ranking government official, assistant secretary or higher, especially in Reagan's and both Bush's Departments of Defense, who hadn't had his fingers in the pie. Since it takes at least two to conduct a conspiracy, Boeing's half of the tasty pie was eaten by a former chairman and several of its current board of directors.

Dan spoke of a sophisticated network of conspirators that had been operating for years, gathering information on powerful men who would be instrumental in awarding government contracts. He didn't provide names, but said I would recognize most of them.

"Almost all of them would be familiar to you, Andy. And I've got something fatally damaging, on every one of them. That's how Boeing got the biggest share of this Star Wars boondoggle."

Dan had looked at me earnestly at that point. "I've been trying to extricate myself from all this for some time. That's why I left Boeing. I've been trying to get out for some time. I thought that I had it all set up, that everyone was persuaded that I wouldn't tell what I know. I was wrong, and now they must think I took something with me, something that would be my protection so they wouldn't kill me. Otherwise they'd just kill me and that would be that."

"So you're saying they want you out of the picture but are afraid you'll blow it all wide open. And that's why they took the kids. For leverage. But why don't you just go ahead and divulge whatever it is they're afraid you're going to divulge?"

"In retrospect, I see I should have. But now that they have our boys, they'll kill them if I do. They would have no reason not to."

It had to admit that made sense. But I still was having difficulty grasping the totality of Dan's story. It was just too fantastic. I couldn't imaging a network so far-reaching and all-encompassing, that someone, somewhere, somehow—someone like Dan, say—wouldn't have divulged something, if only accidentally. Big secrets have a way of unraveling under their own weight. But sometimes they don't. At least that's the theory behind the assassination of President Kennedy, if you believe Oliver Stone. Maybe such a vast network of conspirators could exist.

The trouble was, I couldn't see someone like Dan, a hundred-and-fifty-thousand-dollar-a-year journeyman attorney, being in charge of Boeing's share of the spoils. Why would Boeing trust him that much? I kept waiting for him to explain. He never did.

"So, who's got our boys, Dan?"

His head rocked from side to side in apparent exasperation, but his answer chimed with the clarion ring of truth.

"I can't be sure. But don't trust the FBI, Andy. I know they are in on it, at least some of them are, because I've worked with some agents who helped compile Boeing's files about people in our government. And I know some of those agents are looking for me now."

"Agent Doorham?"

"Don't know him. 'Smith's the guy looking for me."

"The guy who called Jane. Who's Smith?"

"Someone who knows everything."

"Well, God damn it, Dan, what are we supposed to do?!"

"For the moment, nothing. I don't think the boys are in any real danger. Not yet. The boys are the only club they've got, the only thing they can hold over our heads. They're not about to give that up. So for now we wait, until we can figure out a way to get some help. Some help we can trust."

"Like who? If this thing is as big as you say it is…"

"…You can't imagine how big it is, Andy. But there are still a few good men around, a few honest men, and I've got some feelers out…."

"Feelers? Feelers!? Jesus! You talk like this is some kind of executive head-hunt. Damn it, Dan, we're talking about our boys here!"

His face crumpled. My friend the Harvard attorney lowered his face into his hands and shuddered. At that moment, I decided that Dan and I were on the same side. I would trust Dan Crawford. Whether I believed all of what he was telling me or not, I would trust him.

"No one loves his son more than I do," he managed, talking beneath a French cuff he was daubing at his eyes. A very dirty French cuff on the sleeve of a very expensive custom shirt that had been worn for too many days.

"I would gladly sacrifice myself, if I thought that would put Danny and Rick and Miguel out of danger. Or if I could just turn the clock back and start over again and not get involved. But I can't. I can't do that." The look he gave me then would have melted the hearts of a jury of Bible-thumpers in a child pornography case.

"Trust me, Andy. You gotta trust me on this. I promise we'll get our boys back."

I said I would, and we parted. We didn't make any definite arrangements to meet again, but Dan said he would have Gatsby, the attorney, get word to me when we could meet safely again. I followed Dan's car back to the highway and as far as the Agate Pass Bridge that connects Bainbridge Island with the Kitsap Peninsula. At that point I turned back and drove home.

When I arrived, I listened to the second ransom message from Rick and felt my blood freeze to the consistency of a cherry Popsicle.

8

Rick's voice sounded like it had three years ago, when his voice was changing. Even the recorder's tiny speaker caught the soprano-ing panic in his voice.

"Please, dad. Do what they say. These guys, these...these...assholes!" The sound of his face being slapped stung my ears.

"They just brought a dog in off the street and showed us what they would do to us if you don't do exactly what they say. They...they...cut off his ears, dad..." His voice broke then, but there was no slapping sound, just Rick's gasping for control.

"...Then they...then they castrated it dad. Right in front of us. The blood...oh God dad...the blood...."

A dial tone ended the call.

"That's it? Nothing else? What are we supposed to do?"

The Bainbridge cop, David Welsh, poured me a cup of coffee, then reached into the inner packet of his Eisenhower-style jacket. He tipped a slug of something clear and strong from a silver flask into my coffee.

"Drink it. You look like you could use it." It helped a little.

Then FBI agent Doorham took charge. Listening to his calm assurances, I almost forgot Dan's warning about the FBI. Almost.

"I've been involved in two dozen kidnappings, Mister Eastman, and almost all of them turned out just fine, except for the kidnappers. Soon enough, they'll call back and state their demands and how we are supposed to meet them. When they do, you can bet we'll do whatever we have to, to get them—and the boys. You can count on that. Your boys will be back in good shape."

"How can you be so certain?"

He looked at me with a studied expression of infinite patience. "If they meant to do damage to the boys, Mister Eastman, or if they thought you doubted their sincerity, you would have already received proof in the mail. A finger or a toe or an ear. You haven't, and that tells us they think you will do as they want."

Agent Doorham raised his eyebrows, making the whites of his eyes fully visible—the intimidating stare of the predator. "You do realize that we are the experts at this, don't you? Because the last thing we want you to do is to run off and try and solve this yourself."

Obviously, Doorham knew of my absence from the house. How much more did he know? Had I been followed when I called Dan from the Jiffy Mart, or when I met him at the old fruit stand? I didn't think so. If I had been, wouldn't Dan have been taken captive?

"You're wondering what I was doing this morning," I said. "I went into town, into Winslow. I just had to get away from here. Away from all this. I went to Waterfront Park and sat in my car."

He seemed satisfied. But I needed to shift the focus of this exchange. "So, we're just supposed to wait here and do nothing until they call again? Or send us a finger or a toe or an ear? Or a head?"

"We're not exactly doing nothing. We have traced this call, for example. It was placed from a phone booth in a shopping center in Santa Monica."

"Santa Monica. The boys are in California?"

"Impossible to say. They could be in Seattle, even right here on the island. The *call* was placed from Santa Monica. We know your son's voice was recorded again for this phone call, just like the first call, so anyone could have played it over a phone from Santa Monica. The fact the call came originated there doesn't mean much, except that there are multiple people involved. We've fingerprinted the phone booth, of course, and we're keeping it under observation, because some of the kidnappers may still be in Santa Monica."

"So there could be a gang—a group of them? Co-conspirators?" For just a moment, his face took on a look of guilty surprise.

But he ignored my comment and continued his spiel about the typical course of the average kidnapping. I kept my mouth shut, thinking he might accidentally betray something that would confirm Dan's warning. But it was just FBI speech number seven, the one reserved for anxious parents. Doorham spoke lovingly of the FBI's record of "successfully resolved cases." As he related tale after tale of successfully resolved cases, my suspicions grew apace. It was all too pat, too rehearsed. He made no mention of our case, this particular kidnapping, of how they would go about rescuing our boys. Not one word that would have personalized his spiel, not one reference to the kids involved. My son, Rick. Dan Crawford's son, Dan Junior. Alice Sharp's son, Miguel. I began to wonder if he even knew their names, much less had any idea why they were kidnapped. It was as if the "why" of this case was of no concern to him, or to the FBI. Then I realized he probably already knew the "why," already knew why the kids were being held.

Then, almost as if he was reading my mind, Doorham did get personal.

"Can you think of any reason why Rick, Dan Junior, and Miguel would be abducted from the cabin?" His stare returned as he waited for me to answer.

I didn't look away. I knew this had to be a test, that someone with something to hide wouldn't be able to hold his gaze. "It has to have something to do with Dan's...with Dan Senior's disappearance," I said.

"Why?"

"That's why we were there at the cabin in the first place," I said. "I told you that. We were looking for Dan and we half-expected to find him hiding out there. He wasn't, but we did see that someone had slept in the bed—probably Dan—and we found tire prints that looked like they might have been made by Dan's Jeep."

"So you were looking for Dan Crawford, Senior. And as I understand from what you told Captain Able of the Port Angeles Police, you figure someone must have followed you and the boys to the cabin. Why would they do that?"

"Isn't that obvious?" I said. "At that point, the people who killed Dan hadn't found him yet, so they followed us, hoping we would lead them to him."

"And then when you left them alone, they took Rick, Miguel and Dan's son, presumably to pressure Crawford Senior into doing what they wanted him to do, or something. But you have no idea who it was, what they wanted with Dan Crawford. Or why."

He paused. "Is that about it?"

I nodded.

"But why would someone be looking for Crawford? Was he in trouble of some kind? Did he owe someone a lot of money or something? Gambling debts at the Clearwater Casino, maybe?"

"Your guess is as good as mine," I said. "All I know is that Jane Crawford asked me to find out what was going on with Dan, because she was worried about him. She said he was behaving differently since he had been fired, not talking to her, disappearing, sometimes for days at a time. I wasn't able to find out anything, but I figure it has to have something to do with his being let go as a contract negotiator for Boeing." I stopped there, offering nothing more, wondering if Doorham would take my bait and show some reaction.

He didn't. "Can you think of any other reason why the boys were kidnapped—some reason besides whatever was going on with Dan Crawford Senior, I mean."

"Like what?"

"Well, for example, are *you* in any kind of trouble? Has anyone made any threats against you? Do you own money to anyone?"

"Well of course I owe money. Who doesn't? But I don't think American Marine Bank or Visa kidnaps your kids to make sure you pay your bills on time." I smiled at him. "Which I do, by the way."

He managed a smile back. "Glad to hear it. How about the kids themselves. What about Miguel Sharp? His family is wealthy, are they not?"

"Yeah, his grandparents—Alice's parents—are billionaires by now, probably...."

"Miguel's father is involved in the drug trade in Mexico, correct?"

I laughed out loud. "Involved in the drug trade? You gotta be kidding. Because he sells hash pipes and rolling papers to middle-age hippies, you mean?"

"But he probably knows people who are involved in the drug trade."

"Sure," I said, still chuckling. "All those zoned-out dudes who buy his pipes."

"Still, Miguel does come from money."

"Right."

"And his dad might be involved in drugs."

"So you say."

"So maybe whoever followed you to the cabin wasn't looking for Dan Crawford at all, but were actually looking for a chance to abduct

Miguel Sharp so they could get a big ransom from Miguel's grandparents."

"And they took Rick and Dan Junior just because they happened to be there too," I said. "Is that what you're saying?"

"I'm saying it's a possibility."

"Then we're dealing with some really dumb kidnappers, Agent Doorham."

"Why do you say that?"

"Because Miguel Sharp and my son, Rick just took long bus rides, all by themselves, to and from Bend for a summer camp. Anywhere along the way, kidnappers following Miguel Sharp would have had all kind of chances to nab Miguel."

"A summer camp. In Bend. When was this?"

"They left last week and returned a couple days later."

"A couple days? Sounds like a short camp."

"They didn't like it and came home early."

"By themselves, you say. They were travelling alone."

"Yup, just the two of them."

"Alone."

"Well, I'm sure there were other people on the bus."

Doorham waved his hands, as if dismissing the topic. "Okay, I see what you mean. They probably weren't after Miguel. Makes sense. It's got to have something to do with Dan Crawford. And something to do with Boeing."

Once again, his eyes probed mine.

"That's the only thing I can figure out," I said. "I just wish I knew what."

Doorham seemed satisfied with my response, so I turned away and went out on the deck for a smoke. Doorham and Officer Welch stayed inside. I had much to think through, and none of it made much sense. Doorham's earlier bland assurances—and his red herring assertion that the kidnappers were actually after Miguel—seemed to add weight to Dan's story. And yet Dan's tale still seemed so fantastic that I was having trouble accepting it as the truth.

Em finally called at two o'clock, while I was still on the deck. Doorham answered the phone. Em must have been puzzled, for he would tell her nothing about who he was or why he was answering our phone. He just asked for her number and said I would call her right back.

I used the black phone. Em answered before the first ring finished.

"Andy? What's going on? Who was that?"

"Honey..." Christ, I didn't know what to tell her. Anything I said would be horrible to hear. I tried to be reassuring, of course. And of course I wasn't. How do you tell your wife that your child has been kidnapped?

"Darling, I have bad news, about Rick."

"Ohmigod! Is he hurt? What's happened?"

"No, he's okay. He's not hurt, it's just that he's been...he's been kidnapped."

There was a gasp, then a pause. For a moment I thought Em had fainted dead away.

Then, shakily, "Kidnapped. Did you say kidnapped?!"

"Yeah, honey, it's true. Dan Junior and Miguel were taken, too. And...and it's all my fault."

"Oh, God, Andy. Miguel, too?" I could hear her talking to someone else, probably Alice Sharp, Miguel's mom.

Em came back on the phone. "*What*, I mean, *how*, I mean *where* did it happen? The camp in Bend?"

"It happened yesterday. We were trying to find DJ's father. He's been missing...We went to Port Angeles..."

"Port Angeles? I thought the boys were at camp in Bend."

"They came back early. See, we were trying to find Dan Crawford, whose gone missing, and the Crawfords have a cabin near Port Angeles, up in the woods, and we thought Dan might be hiding up there, and we were looking for him, and..."

"But how did the guys get kidnapped?"

"I...I...left them alone, honey. In the cabin...While I went to get something I'd forgotten...."

"And while you were gone, somebody took them."

"Yeah. Oh, God, darling, I'm so sorry. That I didn't stay with the guys...that...."

"I know," she said. And of course she did. She knew exactly how I felt. Then *she* tried to comfort *me*. That's the kind of woman I'm married to. Thank God we were still married. Maybe...If we could get through this....

We talked for only a little longer. Em said she and Alice would get back home as soon as they could. Agent Doorham handed me a slip of paper and I read it to Em: go to the police station; a helicopter would fly them to Bainbridge Island.

And so we said our good-byes and I love you's, brave words, vital words for both of us. Words of hope I clamped onto like a pit bull.

I poured myself a cup of coffee and walked back out on the deck. The coffee burned my throat like it was acid. Part of me wished it was. I walked out to the most distant point of the deck, the part that's cantilevered way out over the beach—at least eight feet out beyond the edge of the seawall. When a high tide and big waves coincide—not an infrequent occurrence—the waves would slam into the seawall and splash up though the deck. The deck had become springy out there at its far reaches, its support a bit rotten from exposure to salty splashes over the years; I still needed to get that fixed, I remember thinking. If you jump up and down, that tip of the deck feels a bit like a diving board, albeit a diving board surrounded by a railing. I found myself recalling the familiar treachery of a diving board made from a weathered pine plank that hung out from the Knife River bridge spanning the swimming hole of my Mora, Minnesota youth, so many years ago, back when I was Rick's age, thirty years ago. Probably that old plank had rotted away by now, along with my youth.

I bounced up and down, wanting to be fifteen again. I bounced on my remembered diving board and the deck bounced back, as if it were trying to help me get my wish. As if the act of bouncing could work magic. As if bouncing was the secret formula for getting the boys back. For restoring my son to me, here and now.

I lowered my head to the rough railing on my magical diving board and wept. It wasn't working.

An hour and a half later, an Orcas Island Medevac helicopter landed in the parking lot next to the house. Agent Doorham brought Em and Alice up to date, verbally reprising the FBI's success, and his own, in solving kidnapping cases. I held my tongue.

Later, as Alice fussed around the kitchen creating dinner from whatever she could find in the cupboard, I pulled Em aside.

"There's something I want you to know, but we can't tell the FBI."

She started to say something but I held my hand to her lips. "No, honey. Say nothing. We'll go somewhere where we can talk."

Em returned to the kitchen and whispered something to Alice. Alice's response was immediate.

"That's okay. You guys go ahead and go out. I understand. I'll be fine. I'll just stay here and fix something to eat for me and these guys."

I looked up a phone number in the Poulsbo directory and told agent Doorham where he could reach us.

Fifteen minutes later, Em and I were at the Sands Restaurant in Poulsbo. I used their phone to check in with Doorham. No new messages had arrived and he would call us at the Sands if any did. Em and I sat in the corner booth farthest from the bar, farthest from the country band that was practicing a tear-jerker of a song about long and winding roads, lost loves, and manifold manifestations of unrequited lust. The Sands was our favorite place when we craved anonymity. Few islanders were likely to see us there, especially now that the dinner rush was over and the crush of drinkers hadn't yet arrived.

I had told Em what I knew while we were driving to the cafe. Neither of us mentioned her "I'm gone" note, nor our abbreviated separation. All the causes of our difficulties still remained, and I knew we'd have to address them. But we didn't talk about those issues, because none of them seemed important now. Our focus was entirely on what we had been most successful in producing together: our son, and what we could do get him back safely, along with Miguel and Dan Junior.

"Do you think Dan's telling the truth?" Em asked.

"Yes. I do." Until that point, I didn't know for sure. Still, I hedged my endorsement. "I don't think he told me everything he knows, but I think the basic story is true."

"The part about the FBI, too?"

"Especially that part. Did you notice that whenever Doorham is talking, he speaks mostly in generalities? He's only once mentioned the specifics of this case, and that was mostly in an attempt to find out what I might know—and then to try and shift my attention to Miguel being the most likely target of the kidnappers, because of their family money."

"That's ridiculous. Isn't it?" Em looked unsure. "I mean, I suppose being from a wealthy family could make someone a tempting target, but why would kidnappers follow all of you guys all the way out to Port Angeles? Hell, they could have nabbed Miguel anytime. It's not like Alice keeps him under lock and key at home in Portland. He walks to and from school every day."

"Exactly. That's what I told Doorham—except I suggested a more logical place to kidnap Miguel would have been when he and Rick were on their way to Bend for camp. Or on the way back. For hours, they were all alone and could have been snatched at any number of bus stops. No, darling, I don't trust the FBI at all. Especially, I don't trust Doorham. He gives me the creeps, and I know he's involved in this whole damn mess with Dan."

"Okay, so what can we do? Is there anything we *can* do?"

"Yeah, I think so. We can keep our eyes on Doorham, for one thing, and see what we can find out by keeping our ears open. Eventually, he might say something revealing. You and Alice can do that."

"Okay. What are you going to do?"

"I'm going to go see Gatsby, Dan's lawyer. That slime-ball knows something, or Dan wouldn't be using him as a go-between. He probably knows where Dan is staying, for one thing, and I'll make him tell me if I have to...I don't know. Whatever I have to do."

"Well, that's a start. Better than just sitting around, worrying ourselves to death. More than we are already. Should we tell Alice about this?"

"I think we have to. She has as much at stake as we do. She can handle it. You don't raise a teenager by yourself without developing some pretty good coping skills."

"What about Mommie Dearest?"

"I'm not sure, but I don't think so. I've been asking myself the same question. So far, I haven't told her about meeting Dan because he was so adamant about me not telling her, and she seems so fragile."

"Okay. We won't tell her anything yet. But if we can verify anything about the FBI, then we should, definitely. Until then, I agree. Jane's got more on her plate than she can handle."

It wasn't until we got back to the house that I remembered that not everything in our world was bleak and forlorn. I remembered my "good news." So I gathered everyone around the kitchen eating bar and told them about my meeting with Juanita Wardell and Chris Noble. It was nice to think about something pleasant and happy for a change.

"We'll celebrate tomorrow, Andy," Em said. "Steaks, baked potatoes, salad, a quart of Roquefort, the whole high-cholesterol binge."

"Great," I said. "How does everyone like their steak?"

Em, Alice and officer Welsh chose medium.

"Rare," said agent Doorham. "Red and juicy. Sometimes I think I must have been born in a cave. But I'll try not to growl and beat my chest. I mean, it is your celebration, Andy, not mine."

He winked at me and at that moment I wanted to snarl and tear him to pieces. He had no business calling me Andy. None at all. But I smiled nicely. Two could play that game.

9

I beat Garfield Gatsby to his office the next morning. Upon seeing me in his law firm's tastefully appointed lobby, he glared at the receptionist, who merely shrugged. So he turned back to me. "I don't recall that we had an appointment, Mister Eastman. And I don't know why we would. I have nothing more for you."

He moved toward his office, saying "Hold my calls, Allison, and let me know as soon as Mr. Powell arrives." He opened the door to his office, walked to a closet hidden behind what I had thought was a seamless wall of solid teak, removed his dark blue pin-striped suit coat, arranged the coat very carefully on a shaped wooden hanger, and hung it in the closet. The closet door closed on hinges recently oiled.

He appeared startled and more than a little irritated that I'd followed him into his lair. I closed the door behind me, quietly and moved to a client chair in front of his desk, while I watched him re-open the closet , re-don his suit coat, and assume his position of power behind his desk. He shot his cuffs as he sat down. I noticed the seat of his chair was a few inches higher than mine. I found the whole display of undressing, redressing, and power-sitting mildly amusing. For my part, I would keep my mouth closed until he was uncomfortable enough to talk. I was getting good at that.

"I suppose you are seeking more information about Mister Crawford." I gave him a nod. "As I said, I have nothing more for you. If I did, I would not be able to divulge it because of…"

"Lawyer-client privilege."

"Precisely."

"Tell me, Garfield, what does 'lawyer-client' have to say about complicity to commit a felony? Felonies, I should say—plural. Just speaking in general terms, say." His portly face morphed through an array of facial displays that would have done Dom DeLuise proud: surprise, amusement, and incredulity—before setting on disgust, an emotion the ever-affable DeLuise could never seem to achieve.

"Surely you are not accusing me of being an accessory to some sort of crime." His dismissive huff was exhaled through his nose, somehow. I resumed my impression of Gary Cooper.

"Because if you are, I assure you that you are most mistaken. Mister Crawford is a client, nothing more." I kept my mouth closed. So far my approach to conversation seemed to be working fine.

"That is to say, he is a client who asked me to convey certain information to you, and I did so, nothing more." I continued to wait. Then I waited some more. And some more. To look at me, you would wonder what I was thinking, what scathing comeback would emerge from my lips.

"Okay," I said. "I see I should I should have followed my first impulse. I should have gone directly to the authorities instead of seeing you, because you've made it clear that you are indeed involved with whatever your 'client' is doing. I'm not sure exactly what that entails, but so far it includes extortion and kidnapping."

His eyes got big. I continued. "It hardly seems appropriate for an 'officer of the court' to withhold knowledge of felonies now in progress, don't you think? I'm betting the King County Prosecuting Attorney and the FBI will agree."

I noted the color draining from his face as I rose from my chair and headed toward the door.

"Wait," he said. "What is it you want to know?"

"Everything. Everything you know, from the top. Start by telling me why Dan Crawford came to you in the first place."

Gatsby took a deep breath, then another. "I first met him about a year ago, at a Chamber after-hours reception. He introduced himself and said he needed to talk to me in private, in the strictest confidence, as soon as possible."

"And?"

"I agreed to meet him here at my office, early the next morning, before anyone else would be in. When he showed up, he gave me a packet of information that I was to keep for him in our safe—a sealed manila envelope that I did not open. He told me to open the envelope and follow the instructions inside only when he told me to, personally. Or in the event of his death."

"Do you still have the envelope?"

"No. I do not. He retrieved it three weeks ago. I have no knowledge of what was inside the envelope. I figured it had to be something he had discovered, probably related to his work at Boeing, perhaps evidence of financial or contract improprieties—something of that nature.

"What did the instructions in the envelope tell you to do?"

"That I was to give the contents of the envelope to...."

His jowls quivered, then sagged, as he heard himself. He spun his chair around and looked out his window at the Federal Building on the next block for half a minute or so. When he'd gotten a grip on himself, at least partly, he turned back.

"I *did* review the contents of the envelope. I felt I needed to. I could not allow the firm to be involved in something that might have been illegal, or even potentially illegal. The instructions in the envelope said I was to give its contents to a certain individual, a member of one of our federal agencies."

"Who?"

"Whom. The pronoun is an object of an understood prepositional phrase. Whom is the proper form."

"I stand corrected. To whom were you to give the envelope?"

"It doesn't matter. The intended recipient is now deceased."

"Dead? When did he die?"

"The day before Crawford picked up the envelope."

"Who died? Who was to receive the envelope?"

"I can't say."

"Why? You just told me you were to give the envelope to someone. I want to know his name."

"The instructions in the envelope said I was never to tell anyone who I had given the envelope to..."

"You mean, 'to whom I was to give the envelope.' Don't end sentences with prepositions, either. Bad form. Anyway, what's the difference? The man's dead. Whom are you protecting, besides yourself?"

"No, no, it's not like that."

"Oh, let's leave it for the moment. Tell me what was in the envelope, besides the instructions."

"Several small sheets of microfilm. They looked like photographic negatives, with many individual pictures on each of a dozen or so pieces of film. Each piece of film was about three inches by five inches.

I couldn't read the images without a viewer, so I don't know their content. When I held one up to the light, I could see what looked like many pages of text. Letters, maybe. Something divided into paragraphs and lists, anyway. Perhaps memos or reports of some sort."

"You didn't get a viewer to check them out?"

"I tried. Our library has a microfilm viewers but not the right kind. I couldn't make it work for that kind of microfilm."

"So you have no idea of the content of these microfiches?"

"Fishes? Micro-fishes? Is that what they're called?"

"Feeeshes. Micro-*feeeshes*. A microfilm contains one image on each frame of regular movie-type film—one picture or one page of text or data per frame. The images on a microfiche are much smaller, so there are multiple pages on a single piece of three-inch by five-inch film. Both microfilm and microfiche are falling out of favor. Most everyone scans documents directly into computer files now."

"Oh." His stupidity seemed genuine.

So there we were. I now knew as much as Gatsby knew, which was something, but not much. I did know that microfilms and microfiches were still in use at Boeing, simply because hundreds of thousands of pages of Boeing technical and legal documents had already been thus recorded, and the process of scanning their images into readable and reproducible computer files was time-consuming, and therefore expensive.

Listening to Gatsby, I concluded the microfiches Dan had given him for safe-keeping probably contained lists of people involved in the Boeing conspiracy. But Gatsby had not read the lists, nor would he tell me who was to receive the microfiches if Dan died. Not that it mattered much at the moment. The man who was intended to receive them could have told me, but he was dead and unable to enlighten me or anyone else. So apparently the microfiches still were in Dan's possession.

At least now I knew what the kidnappers were looking for—and what I had to find if I had any hope of getting the boys back: Dan Crawford—and his microfiches.

"Where is Dan Crawford now?"

"I won't tell you that. He made me swear not to tell anyone."

I reached across the desk and picked up the phone and punched seven numbers. He snatched the phone from my hand and put it back on its base. "What do you think you're doing?"

"Calling the FBI. Specifically, Special Agent Doorham, at my house." I lied, of course. I'd punched seven random numbers. No way was I going to tell Doorham anything.

"Oh, very well," Gatsby said. "Perhaps it's best if you saw Mister Crawford yourself. He is staying at the Edgewater Inn, under an assumed name."

"What name?"

"Rick Eastman."

Jesus. My son's name. I was beginning to hate Dan Crawford.

"What room number?"

"I don't know. I would tell you if I did. Now, if that is all, I want you to leave. I've told you everything I know."

"Except the name of the man who was to get the envelope."

"Does it matter? The man is dead. He can't tell you anything."

"Exactly. The man is dead. So tell me his name. Or tell it to Agent Doorham."

"Commander Joseph Bottoms, U.S. Coast Guard."

"The guy who fell overboard in that rescue attempt?"

"That's correct."

It had been in all the papers and all over the TV. There was a good deal of confusion about what had happened. A sailboat caught in a storm on Puget Sound had capsized, and another boat had radioed an SOS to the Coast Guard. Commander Bottoms had been performing a readiness inspection aboard a Coast Guard cutter at the Coast Guard pier when the call came in and he had jumped at the chance to accompany the crew on a rescue mission. When the cutter reached the capsized boat, the Coasties had found no trace of its crew.

Somehow, during the ensuing search, Bottoms had fallen overboard, his absence unnoticed until the cutter had towed the empty sailboat to the pier. A subsequent all-out search had failed to turn up Bottoms' body. It was found a couple days later by a groundskeeper at Seattle's West Point sewage treatment plant; the body had washed ashore during a higher than average high tide. By then, seals, gulls, and other hungry critters had mangled all evidence of foul play, if there had been any.

Nearly as mysterious as Bottom's death was the fact that no one had ever come forward to claim the boat that had capsized. It had been registered just a week earlier in the name of an unemployed logger from Shelton who had never, he said, been near the water, and who barely had enough money to make the payments on his five-year old pickup, much less splurge on something so purely recreational as a sailboat.

The consensus of the media was that the boat had been stolen for use in a drug run and that the thief or thieves had forged the boat's registration as a precautionary hedge. I remember thinking that the episode sounded like a promising beginning for a novel.

"Bottoms worked in the Federal Building?"

"Yes. On the seventeenth floor. Right over there."

I followed his outstretched arm and looked toward what I assumed was the window of the local Coast Guard office, where my eyes met the gaze of a uniformed man standing in the window, looking my way with binoculars. I wondered if he had been reading our lips.

When I left Gatsby's office a few minutes later, I looked out toward the Coast Guard window again. No one was standing there, and the vertical blinds had been closed.

10

This was almost too easy. I'd conned Garfield Gatsby into divulging everything he knew. Now, all I had to do was discover which room at the Edgewater Dan was occupying and I would add "detective" to my tech-writing resume, should anyone ever need a semi-literate detective. By the time I reached the motel, I knew just how to proceed.

Approaching the Edgewater's front desk as if I lived in the place, I said, "I've misplaced my room key. Do you have another? I'm Rick Eastman."

The clerk checked his computer screen and handed me a key. I glanced at the fob as I approached the elevator. Bingo. Room 214. I stifled the urge to hold my fist aloft in victory. But I may have mouthed "Yes!" in the elevator.

Dan's room was on the water side of the hallway, about two-thirds of the way to its end. A *DO NOT DISTURB* sign hung from the doorknob. I knocked anyway, now a full-fledged Spenserian detective with all the wit and none of that tedious brawn and suspicious cooking talent. No one came to the door, so I let myself in. I hoped I wouldn't have to wait long for Dan's return.

The door swung open on a darkened room, the lights off, the drapes pulled. The air conditioner was on, the room cold as a tomb.

Dan's body lay face-down between the bed and a prehistoric pair of prefab Danish *moderne* chairs in front of the window. Someone had stuck a gun in Dan's left ear and pulled the trigger. The right side of his head was gone, the drapes catching much of the gore, most of the rest congealed under what was left of his head.

I didn't see a gun near either of Dan's hands, which probably ruled out suicide. But I did find something else that made me pass out before I had a chance to throw up.

Clutched tightly in Dan's dead right hand was someone's ear.

When I came to, I didn't know where I was, but something was wrong. My hands seemed to be fastened together behind my back and someone was wrestling me to my feet. I was spun around, roughly by my capturer, a stout fellow with eye-watering B.O., a dour look on his face, and the smell of too many cigars on his breath.

From behind me, somewhere over by the door to the room, a familiar voice said, "Yes, officers, that's the man who claimed to be Mister Eastman. He said he had lost his key, so I gave him one, but Muriel, she's the afternoon maid, Muriel said she knew Mister Eastman and this wasn't him, but by then he was on the elevator so I called nine-one-one."

Oh, Jesus. Dan was dead and the police thought I was the killer. "But I am Mister Eastman," I said, saying the dumbest, yet only true thing I could think of.

"You have the right to remain silent," said the officer holding me. "Anything you say can be used as evidence against you…"

"I want my lawyer. Right now. Garfield Gatsby. In the Norton Building. His card's in my wallet."

The cop fished my wallet out of my hip pocket and found the card. Then he spoke to someone via the radio clipped to his collar.

"They'll call him for you," he said. "He can meet you at the station."

Gatsby made it to the station before we did. He did not look happy to see me, much less to have been identified as my lawyer.

"Did you kill him?" he asked. "Did you shoot him when he didn't tell you what you wanted to know?" If looks could kill, Gatsby's gaze would put the lethal injection folks out of business. Looked like my lawyer wasn't counseling silence.

I agreed to make a statement to the police, while Gatsby sat by, no doubt hoping I would say something incriminating so he could plea-bargain his way out of my life forever. I told the police everything I could remember—many times, interrupted by many questions. After an hour, someone finally called my home and spoke to Special Agent Doorham.

"You can go, Mister Eastman. Doorham backs up your story, and the preliminary report from our forensics people says it looks like Crawford was dead for several hours before you found him."

"Whose ear was he holding?"

"His own. They think whoever shot him cut off his ear first. Probably to make him divulge something." I closed my eyes and slumped lower in the chair, offering a short but heart-felt prayer of thanks.

"Mister Eastman?" I looked into the detective's eyes, which looked warmer than they had a moment ago. "How about leaving this to the experts—to us and the FBI? Will you do that?"

"Yeah, I will. Of course. Believe me, I've learned my lesson."

Like hell I would.

I called Em.

"I know. Jane called me right after the police called her. Are you okay?"

"Yeah, I'm all right. The cops will get me home. Any other news from your end?"

"Nothing. Hurry home, Andy. Please."

When the Seattle detective and I arrived, we joined the crowd that had gathered in the house. A third ransom call had arrived just a few moments before my ferry docked. Agent Doorham had been taking a dump in the bathroom and Em had answered the phone. It was Rick's voice again, another recording.

"Dad! They've killed DJ's dad and they still don't have what they want. Please, dad, if you know what they're looking for, give it to them. They are going to kill Deej next, then Miguel, then me..."

Rick's voice broke off, as if the microphone had been yanked from his hand. Then there was the sound of a big man's heavy breathing. Then a voice from a "Godfather" out-take. "Godfather III," probably. A really bad imitation of a hood.

"You have information that belongs to us, Mister Eastman. We will contact you in two days with instructions."

Doorham had reached the phone just in time to see Em slump to the floor in a faint. He called the medics immediately, but she came around before they arrived.

Now the medics were refusing to leave, saying they needed to make sure Em was all right. One of them was attempting to put a pressure cuff on her arm to get a blood pressure reading.

"Get away from me, you twit! Go away. Let me talk to my husband." The medics backed off and soon departed. You do not get in my wife's face when she does not want you in her face.

"It will be all right, honey," I said. Then I said it again. And again, as I held her close. I hoped she believed me. I wished I did.

Alice joined us, looking more composed than either Em or me, and we walked out on the deck to get away from the massed hoards of officialdom jostling each other in the kitchen and dining room. The Seattle detective was giving Special Agent Doorham and Bainbridge PD Officer Welch holy hell for keeping him in the dark. Doorham was defending himself. Welch just shrugged, as if to say, "not my deal."

I was sick of all of them, except maybe the Bainbridge officer, David Welch. His presence had been reassuring, his manner considerate. He had no official ax to grind. He was great. But everyone else pissed me off. I marched back in and ordered all of them out of my house, except Welch.

The Seattle detective left, telling Doorham that he would be in touch later. "I'll be talking to your Seattle resident agent, Doorham."

"Then you'll be talking to me. I *am* the Seattle Resident Agent." I could hear the capital letters in his voice, which infuriated me.

"I said you're fired, Doorham! Get out of here! Now!"

"You can't fire me, Mister Eastman. The FBI has jurisdiction of all kidnappings. Kidnappings are a federal, not a local police responsibility."

"Not this time. This isn't just kidnapping Doorham. It's murder now, and I don't want you or any of your goons involved. Get out of my house, or I'll have Officer Welch here arrest you for trespass."

"I understand that you are upset, Mister Eastman. You have every reason to be. But, really, I must remain here. I have no choice. I need to coordinate our efforts to get your son back, and the Sharp boy, and the Crawford kid."

I took a deep breath and shuddered it out. Then yielded, which must have come as a surprise to him.

"Okay," I said, willing myself to appear calm. "Come out here with me, then. You need to see something."

I moved toward the farthest point of the deck, feeling my diving-board deck bounce a little under the weight of my steps. Doorham followed, no doubt puzzled by my sudden change of heart. Taking the hint, Em and Alice kept Officer Welch occupied in the house, asking him questions.

I leaned over the railing, noting the tide was out. A few clams were busy creating little suck-holes in the gravel-studded sand fifteen feet below me. Doorham followed me to the railing and, like a dummy— monkey see, monkey do—leaned over the railing.

Crouching quickly, I grabbed his crotch with my right hand and the belt of his pants with my left, then heaved him up and shoved with all my strength.

The railing broke under his weight and Doorham toppled over and fell to the beach, landing on his hands, but mostly on his head. I heard his neck crunch, a queerly musical snare-drum riff in perfect cadence with the martial music filling my head.

"That's for Dan, you miserable son of a bitch. And for our boys, too."

I don't think he heard me.

11

Pandemonium. But no one arrested me. Apparently, only Em and Alice had witnessed the event; Officer David Welch's back was to the windows. Only Em, Alice, Doorham and I knew the truth. Well, Doorham too, but he wasn't talking, being unconscious. He had survived, damn it all.

Just to show you that my heart is in the right place, right after I descended the steps, hopped onto the beach, and kicked Doorham in the ribs, I directed his rescue effort. I called 9-1-1 and when the medics arrived, told them to take Doorham to a hospital. Any hospital. Anybody would have thought I actually cared.

"Be careful of his neck," I said. "Wouldn't want to see him paralyzed for life."

They strapped him to a stretcher, loaded him in their van and left, siren wailing.

After awhile, everyone left, except David Welch, the local cop, now the defacto representative of law enforcement. He stationed himself by the phone while Em, Alice, and I strolled along the beach. They wondered—to put it mildly—why I had thrown Doorham off the deck.

"Because he's responsible for the kidnapping. And Dan's murder."

"What?!" was Alice's response. Although Em had told her of our suspicions, Alice still clung to the normal, rationale belief that the FBI doesn't do assassinations and that all G-men are good guys, notwithstanding the heritage of J. Edgar Hoover and systematic Bureau wiretapping and harassment of law-abiding citizens whose only offense was to protest some of the many shameful policies and actions of their own government. For that matter, Em too wasn't all that convinced of the truth of what Dan had told me about the FBI's part in Boeing's scheme.

But *I* was convinced, and I can be damned persuasive. Right then I needed to be. I needed to be right about Doorham's role, especially. Otherwise my actions were *prima facie* evidence of lunacy. While I knew I was maxed out on stress, I was pretty sure I was still sane. Not completely, maybe, but rational enough to convince Em and Alice that Agent Doorham needed to be off the case, even if my method of removal had been a bit extreme.

Then I told them what Gatsby had told me about the microfiches, and I talked about Coast Guard Commander Bottoms' recent and highly suspicious death.

"It's obvious that Dan trusted Commander Bottoms. It's also obvious that someone else figured that out too—and killed Bottoms to get him out of the picture."

"And now they've killed Dan," Em said. "Who's next, Andy? Us? Our boys?"

"I don't think so. Not until they've got those microfiches, anyway. Which means we've got to get them before they do."

We strolled the beach for half an hour, trying to sort things out. We were sure of some things now, mostly that the folks we were dealing with were ruthless; they'd do anything to prevail, or at least to minimize their exposure. They would stop at nothing. They'd already killed Dan and they probably had killed Commander Bottoms too, and now they had our boys.

We concluded that we needed to focus on understanding the events leading up to their kidnapping. Then maybe we'd be able to figure out what to do.

This much we knew: that Dan had recovered the microfiches he'd given to Gatsby for safekeeping, We knew that his murderers still hadn't found the microfiches, or we wouldn't have gotten that phone call from the guy pretending to be a mobster. Which meant Dan must have hidden them pretty well after retrieving them from Gatsby's safe. I pointed out that items as small as thin-film three-inch by five-inch microfiches could be hidden almost anywhere, even tucked into a book somewhere. But where?

For sure, we needed to find the microfiches; without them, we had no bargaining chip at all—no way to negotiate for the release of our boys.

Em asked the obvious question. "So what now?"

"We've got to find those microfiches. I'm sure they list the folks Dan was blackmailing on Boeing's behalf."

"Can we do that? Where do we start looking?" Alice asked.

"I don't have a clue. But we'll figure it out. We have to."

Em said, "Well, at least now we know what we're looking for."

Finally, I had an idea that felt brilliant in its simplicity. "Wait a second. We know the kidnappers are looking for Dan's microfiches, right? Well, without a viewer to actually see what's on it, it's pretty hard to tell one microfiche from another."

Em caught my drift immediately. "So all we need are any old microfiches?"

I hugged her tightly. "You got it. All we have to do is make the kidnappers believe that we have what they're looking for. I'll get some microfiches from the tech library at work, and then we can set up a trap."

Alice interrupted. "Can't we let the cops handle that?"

"Which cops?" I said. "We know we can't run down to the hospital and tell Doorham our plan and let him work out the details."

"Oh, yeah. Sorry. Until we see whose names are on the microfiches, we can't be sure who is involved, can we? I keep forgetting that. Jesus. So who do we trust?"

"At this point? Just ourselves, guys," I said. "We'll have to do this by ourselves."

"Can we?" Em looked a little shaky.

"Of course," I said, feeling more self-confidence that I probably should have. Tossing a 200-pound bad guy off my balcony seemed to have engorged my testes. "And we will. Don't worry. We'll make it work."

Officer Welch looked at us with concern as we walked in. Maybe it was the look of grim determination on our faces.

"You guys all right?"

I shrugged. "No. But we will be soon."

Alice pulled a big jug of Gallo Blush out of the refrigerator. It was half full. I hadn't been the only one who needed a drink that day. Alice filled four glasses to the brim, then reached back into the refrigerator and pulled out four huge steaks.

"T&C had a sale on T-bones today. As I recall, we were going to celebrate tonight."

I'm sure officer Welch though we were celebrating my success as a soon-to-be-published writer. And maybe we were, a little.

But mostly we were celebrating because we finally had a plan. Not a complete plan, but at least the rough outline of one. Fleshed out, and with a little luck, we might get our boys back. Maybe pretty soon.

"To us," I said, raising my glass. "And our boys. And to Dan's memory."

Our first order of business the next morning was to call on Jane Crawford. We intended it to be a sympathy visit, pure and simple. After knocking on the front door and getting no response, we opened it. Through the double French doors at the back of the house, we could see Mommie Dearest on the deck. She was just standing there, immobile, as if someone had Super-Glued her feet to the deck. As we moved to through the French doors, I could see she was staring out at the gravel bar that closed off their little cove at low tide, studying something only she was seeing: her dead husband's body sprawled on a hotel room floor.

She hadn't seen us and she hadn't heard us knocking on her front door or opening the back door. She was hearing nothing over her torrent of grief and despair.

Em touched her ever so lightly on the shoulder. Jane jerked, as if slapped.

"Oh! Hi, Em. Can I get you some iced tea? Oh, hello, Andy, Alice. How nice to see you. Would you like some too?" She looked back in the house, as if seeing someone there. "I'll get some for Dan, too."

Then she returned from whatever planet she was visiting and collapsed into a deck chair.

"Oh God, what's wrong with me?! Dan's not ever going to want anything, is he? What am I going to do, Em? What am I going to do?!"

I couldn't hear Em's response as she murmured into Jane's ear. She knelt close, holding her tightly, tears streaming down her face, too. They rocked back and forth, wedded in sorrow.

I'd never felt more like a foreigner, a visitor to a world whose customs I understood but, at that moment could only observe. I don't know how Alice felt, but we both retreated to the house. Alice found a pitcher of tea already chilling in the refrigerator. I located some tall glasses, clacked them full of ice from the spout on the freezer door, then set the glasses next to the pitcher on a metal tray decorated with neon-blue fishes and blaze-orange starfish and juggled the whole festive party scene out to the deck.

"Okay, you guys," Alice said, handing each of them a cloth napkin. "Enough of that. You'll water down the Lipton's Instant."

As sometimes happen in times of extreme grief, we laughed. A way of affirming our humanity, I suppose. Or just the simple fact that we four, at least, were still alive, and while we were alive we still had hope. We each had a tall glass of tea, then a refill. We didn't talk a lot. We didn't need to. For the moment, we just needed to be with each other.

Jane broke the silence. "You know the worst thing about all this? It's that I don't understand anything. Nothing makes any sense. I don't have a clue why Dan was killed or why our boys were taken. I can't figure it out and nobody's telling me anything."

I looked at Em for wisdom. She nodded. "It's time," she mouthed silently.

So I told Jane everything we knew, speaking as softly and reassuringly as I could.

Jane kept shaking her head, having trouble focusing on my words at first. Then her attention became rapt. She looked like she wanted to interrupt at several points, but she restrained herself and kept listening until I had finished explaining how her husband of twenty years had become involved in something that had killed him.

"He was killed by the company he helped make rich," she said. "Why, Andy? Why would they do that?"

She deserved an answer; I didn't have it, not all of it anyway. "I can only conclude that Dan was trying to get out of the blackmail business, and I think he made some photographic records to give him some negotiating clout, and somehow that backfired on him."

She shook her head. More of a quiver than a shake, acceptance and rejection at the same time, like she couldn't believe it but had no choice. I hoped I had proffered something that wasn't completely awful as a memory of her husband: that Dan Crawford, ever-stalwart father and ever-faithful husband, finally had summoned the gumption to do the right thing, to try to get out of and repair the mess he had helped create. That was better than Jane thinking the alternative, that Dan was simply trying to set himself up as a one-man extortion center, holding the goods on everybody involved, Boeing and government co-conspirators alike.

For Jane's sake, I hoped the first scenario, the one I had offered her, was the truth. But I still wondered if the latter scenario might be closer to the mark. While there was no clear evidence that Dan had created the microfiched lists for his own future gain, his story to me that day at the fruit stand, preceded by his assurances during our dinner conversation in this house, assurances that hinted at something that would "come together soon" to solve all their problems—all that sounded like the second scenario. In any event, the blackmailers had already taken their revenge on Dan and they would kill our boys as soon as they had gotten those microfiches. They would bury the boys and all evidence of their involvement in the conspiracy.

So from my standpoint, it didn't matter. Whichever scenario was true, Dan had paid for his sins with his life; what remained was much more important: getting our boys back alive, unharmed.

"Where are the other kids, Jane?" I asked the question more to get my mind off Rick, Miguel and Dan Junior, than out of any real curiosity.

"At Dan's folks' place in Sequim. They will stay there until the funeral. That will be a little while yet, according to the police. They don't know when they'll release his body. Soon, I hope."

"What about you?" Em interjected, trying to shift the talk away from dead bodies. "Do you want to stay with us, so you aren't all alone?"

Jane shook her head slowly, left to right, then back to left.

"No, no, I don't think so. I *am* alone now. And I need to be here when my Danny gets back."

She made it sound like DJ was off at the movies, and I wondered if Jane's grasp of the situation was slipping. Then she finished her thought.

"Sooner or later, those bastards will call, and I need to be here to take their call. Then I will promise to do whatever they want me to do, and then I'll get my Danny back. And then I will hunt them down and kill every last one of them."

Her calmness and absence of emotion meshed with my conviction that all of us would do the same, given half a chance. Hell, I had already begun, by dropping Seattle Resident Agent Doorham on his head.

12

Of the three strangers waiting for us in our living room, only one looked familiar. Officer David Welch could hardly wait to make introductions. "This is Special Agent Chester Griffin of the FBI, Tom MacDonald from the *Seattle Times,* and *this* is Harold Nathan from CBS."

Ah, yes, Harold Nathan: one of Dan Rather's roving reporters. By Officer Welch's demeanor, it was apparent that Harold Nathan and Tom MacDonald had nearly finished interviewing Agent Griffin, and that Welch, figuring he would be next, was a little disappointed we had showed up just then.

After handshakes were exchanged all around, the two journalists excused themselves and returned to the deck to finish with Agent Griffin. A few moments later, Welch replaced Griffin on the deck. A cameraman motioned them to move toward the outer edge of the deck. Puget Sound and the Seattle skyline would make a good backdrop, more scenic than the usual crime scene report with yellow tape fluttering in the background.

While we were observing all this activity, Special Agent Griffin pulled us aside and escorted us into the house. He needed to go over some "protocol issues." Which mostly meant establishing his authority. Despite Agent Doorham's abrupt incapacitation and regardless of our feelings, the FBI would indeed remain in charge of the investigation. The United States Congress, in its wisdom, had given the Bureau "plenary authority to investigate potential interstate crimes, especially those involving the kidnapping of children."

"So I will not tolerate any interference from you or from anyone else, Mister Eastman," he said.

I nodded my understanding. Perhaps it was time to show some compliance.

"Secondly," he continued, "I must insist that you not allow yourselves to be interviewed by any members of the press while our investigation proceeds. To do so could well have serious implications for your boys," he said. "I'm sure you understand."

We were sitting on the sofa in the living room, Em and me. I felt Em stiffen at Griffin's implied threat, and my determination to appear cooperative evaporated in the time it took to clear my throat.

"Tell me, Special Agent-in-Charge Chester Griffin. When you shot Dan Crawford, did it make your binky straight?"

Instantly, a different part of Griffin hardened, his visage resembling those on Mt. Rushmore, only redder, confirming what I suspected: Griffin, like Doorham, was indeed complicit. Maybe he hadn't cut off Dan's ear, and perhaps someone else had pulled the trigger. But Griffin was part of it. He'd been in Dan's hotel room, he'd waited outside, or he'd dispatched the killers. I *knew* that now; his demeanor confirmed it. An innocent man, even a cop trained to maintain his cool, would have reacted vigorously to my accusation. Griffin didn't. He didn't bristle. He didn't yell. His response had been a quickly controlled facial flush. I got the impression he hadn't even been particularly surprised by me calling him a killer, probably because he was knew I could do nothing to prove it. He was a study in glacial calmness.

When he finally spoke, his voice was controlled, his words well-scripted. "No, I did not shoot Mr. Crawford. As to whether Mr. Crawford's killer…enjoyed himself, I wouldn't know." His attempt to look bemused at my accusation needed more rehearsal.

I looked out the sliding door toward the deck. CBS's local-affiliate cameraman was packing his gear, getting ready to leave. Apparently Agent Griffin had already told the press that they would not be allowed to interview Em, Alice, or me. For a heady couple seconds, I toyed with the notion of luring Agent Griffin to the same place on the deck where Agent Doorham had taken his dive. It would be easier the second time, with the railing already busted, and video of Griffin's assisted plunge would make a gang-busters opening for tonight's CBS Evening News.

Griffin interrupted my little fantasy. "I've been talking to Agent Doorham. Claims you threw him off your deck. Not a very charitable thing to do, considering how hard he—all of us—have been working to get your boys back."

"Huh. Funny. That's not my recollection at all. As I recall, he had gotten all swelled up and maybe a little light-headed from all his airy self-regard. Probably made him a little unbalanced out there by the edge of the deck. Or maybe he thought he could walk on water."

"This is not a laughing matter, Mister Eastman."

"Oh. I'm sorry. Was I laughing?"

"Well, there will be a complete investigation, you may be assured of that. Understood? Right. Now let me make one thing perfectly clear."

At that point, I expected the Nixon line: "I am not a crook."

Instead he said, "I *am* in charge of this case, and you will do nothing, repeat, *nothing* to jeopardize our investigation. That is, if you expect to remain a free man—or see your boys alive." In that instant, his facial control lapsed, replaced by an ugliness I hadn't expected.

I didn't respond. I didn't need to. Griffin knew he had made his one point perfectly clear: He *was* a crook. And the FBI's investigation would be not a search for our boys at all, because they already had them. It would be a search for Dan's microfiches. And when the microfiches were found and destroyed, our boys would be disposed of too.

As Griffin moved onto the deck to make sure the fourth estate was departing, I followed him out the sliding door. The cameraman and Tom MacDonald of the *Seattle Times* had already started down the stairs, but Harold Nathan was putting up an argument.

I had to raise my voice to be heard.

"Tell me, Special Agent-in-Charge Chester Griffin. What's your stance on the First Amendment? Is that repealed for the duration of your so-called investigation, too?"

There. Another unrehearsed response. Griffin wheeled and raised his fist in homage to Thor, before he managed to restrain himself and pretend he needed to scratch a sudden itch on his head. Then he spun on his heel and ushered Harold Nathan toward the stairs. Over his shoulder, he told Officer Welch to leave, too. He, Special Agent Griffin, would take the evening shift. Welch looked at me. I raised my eyebrows.

Harold Nathan had reached the landing, halfway down the stairs, where *Seattle Times'* Tom MacDonald had paused when he had overheard my question.

"A moment of your time, please, fellas," I called out. I elbowed my way past Agent Griffin and escorted Nathan and MacDonald down to the parking lot. There, I said a few things to hold their interest, and obtained a promise of cooperation. They left and I returned to the house. I felt good. Really good. I had kicked off the first phase of our plan.

When I returned to the house, I said to Em and Alice, "Come on, guys. We need to eat." As we trooped out, I directed my exit line at Griffin. "Hope you brought a lunch. Not much to eat here, besides your words."

Agent Griffin slid the glass door shut behind us with such force it jumped out of its track, fell onto the deck, and shattered. I shook my head, and wiggled a "tsk-tsk" finger at him.

We looked back from the head of the stairs. Griffin's face was welded to the phone receiver, his mouth working furiously. He probably wasn't ordering pizza.

When we arrived at Farley's, Alice insisted on buying dinner. So I ordered the wine, a large carafe of "Sparkling Rosé," which sounded cheery and hopeful. Alice placed her call from the pay phone in the lobby. A few minutes later she slid into the booth wearing an impish grin. Refilling Em's glass and mine, she poured one for herself and held it high.

"To the boys, and lots of money, and especially to my folks, whose hearts are always in the right place."

"We're all set?" Em said. "Just like that?"

"Yup. The money will be in your account when the bank opens in the morning."

"How much is your dad sending?" I said.

Alice frowned. "Just what he has in his money-market account. Three and a half."

"Thousand," I said.

"No, million, you dummy," she said, happy with her "Gotcha!" "He'll transfer another three and a half by the end of the week, if we need it."

Em said, "Good Lord. I think three and a half million dollars will be plenty."

"Well, Dad said it's no problem sending more. It's looking like this year's grapes will be as exceptional as the last four or five, and the oldest of those Pinot Noirs are just now hitting the shelves. You know my parents, guys. They'll do whatever they can do to help get the boys back. Money's no object when it comes to Miguel. They've just been waiting to hear how they could help."

"Jesus, Alice. I knew your folks had money, but I had no idea," I said, managing to refill my glass without knocking it off the table.

"It's only money, Andy, and it's not worth beans—or grapes— compared to Miguel and Rick. And Dan Junior. And Jane...My God, that poor woman! Is she going to hold up through all this?" Alice directed the question at Em, who nodded tentatively.

"We all will," I said. Em's nod became more vigorous.

Em brought us back to Earth. "Okay. So we've got the money. Now let's figure out what we need to write and get it printed."

We spent three hours at Farley's, eating, talking, writing, rewriting. And emptying another carafe of pink froth in the process. We closed the place, in fact.

I didn't think to inquire about my missing $13.78 money order on the way out. Things really *are* relative.

13

The next morning I told an acutely wary Agent Griffin I needed to go to the bank. As I figured he would, he insisted on accompanying me. Convinced I was up to something, he was not about to let me out of his sight. Griffin called the Bainbridge cop shop and told them to send David Welch out to cover the phone. A few minutes later, Welch arrived and Griffin said we would take his FBI car, a dark blue Ford with fat black-wall tires and tiny painted hubcaps, a stubby antenna on its roof, no markings, and a perfectly anonymous Washington plate. The car screamed "Here come da fuzz, here come da fuzz."

"Which bank?" Griffin said.

"American Marine. Downtown. Take a right at Winslow Way." I offered no other information. Let him think I was covering an over-draft—or withdrawing funds for a ransom. Or about to withdraw microfiches from a safe deposit box.

After a five-minute ride of strained silence, Griffin parked in an angled slot in front of the bank and followed me into the lobby.

Tellers' eyes swiveled towards us. Eyes generally do not swivel my way, but big fund transfers don't happen every day, even on Bainbridge Island. Like the island and its town of Winslow, the bank is small and word travels quickly.

Dick Nelson spotted me as I got in line for a teller and approached, his hand outstretched. I took it, shook it.

It was a sweet moment, being welcomed by Dick Nelson. Everyone called him "the Admiral," for reasons never fully explained but probably because he headed American *Marine* Bank. Could this be the same Dick Nelson who had turned me down for a home improvement loan (repair of a springy deck) just a couple months ago?

"Wanna make sure everything's okay with my account, Dickie." The Admiral stifled a grimace at my familiarity.

"Of course. I'm sure Grace can help you." He led us to a vacant window. "Grace, would you run a copy of Mister Eastman's account statement?" Then he turned toward me, wanting to ask why such a large amount of money had appeared overnight in my account. But he didn't. Breeding tells.

The teller presented the statement with a straight face. I thanked her, then moved toward the door. The Admiral touched my shoulder, ever so gently, like a three-year-old tugging at his mom's skirt.

"About that loan, Andy…"

"Loan? Oh. I don't think so, Dickie. I'm not interested in lending the bank any money just now." I gave him a wink. Had I not, Dickie might have forgotten his breeding and mouthed something more suited to a Marine drill sergeant than the Admiral of American Marine Bank.

I handed Griffin the bank statement as he started the car. He looked at it carefully, his lips spelling the amount silently before repeating it audibly.

"Three and a half million dollars?"

"A million of that can be yours, Agent Griffin."

"You trying to bribe a federal official?"

"Call it that if you want, but I prefer to think of it as a reward for information leading to arrest and conviction. I'm offering you a chance to redeem yourself. A way out of something you don't know how to get out of. Enough money to protect yourself and your family from retaliation from…from whomever you implicate when you talk to King County's Prosecuting Attorney."

"Uh…." His lips clamped shut as he weighed his options: keeping on the current course and keeping his mouth shut, versus the risks of retaliation if he didn't. Could he forego prosecution by turning State's Evidence? Could he get into the WitSec program? Would it be secure enough for him and his family? Would a million dollars make a new life under the Witness Protection Program more palatable? He stared out the window at the front of the bank, probably visualizing things he probably didn't want to see—images I sure as hell didn't want to think about.

"Think about it," I said, sounding more certain than I felt. "And while you're thinking about it, take me to Harrison Hospital in

Bremerton. Just don't think too long, because I will be making the same offer to your colleague."

Grifffin's head swiveled my way so fast you could hear vertebrae engaged in a snappy argument over rights-of-way.

"Of course, the earlier bird gets the fatter worm. First guy to co-operate gets the full million. Second worm—er, bird—gets half as much."

Sporadic police-band calls on the radio were the only interruption to his thoughts and mine as we headed to Bremerton. My thoughts wandered to Em and Alice and how they were proceeding with their parts of our plan. So far, so good, I figured, but I had to wonder if we could pull it off. Most importantly, would Griffin take me up on my offer?

A half-hour later, he loudly cleared his throat as we exited onto Kitsap Way and turned toward the hospital. "Okay, you got a deal."

I reached over and shook his hand and tried for my best John Wayne imitation. "Welcome aboard, pilgrim. But remember, the penalty for desertion is the firing squad."

Doorham, the mostly paralyzed deck diver, snarled at both of us from the loud end of a whole lot of stainless steel and nylon truss-work.

"The fuck you want?"

He meant the question for me, but Agent Griffin answered. "Listen to what he's offering, George. Listen carefully, because I've already accepted."

I hadn't asked for Griffin's help but was grateful for it. I explained the deal to Doorham. "I don't particularly care what you decide," I concluded. "I need only one agent's testimony, and I've already got that."

Doorham's response was blunt. "Go to hell, fuck-face. You too, Chester. You're both dead meat." He glared at me. "You'll live just long enough to lose the suit I'm filing, Eastman. You better buy all the insurance you can with what's left of your money, because I'll own your wife for the rest of her very short and very miserable life. I'll leave her just enough money to bury herself and your son."

Griffin leaned close to his former colleague and said something I couldn't make out. But I sure heard Doorham's response.

"No way. Not a chance in hell."

Griffin's confidence seemed to slip and I wondered if my prize witness was about to renege. Ah well, I could only play the hand I'd dealt myself. I put Garfield Gatsby's card on the steel tray directly in front of Doorham.

"My offer stands until five o'clock, Doorham. Since you're in no shape to dial the phone, have someone call this number for you when you come to your remaining senses."

Doorham took a deep breath and blew the card across the room. Griffin and I left.

"Come on, pilgrim," I said to Griffin as we walked to his car. "You can drop me at the ferry terminal before you head back to the island."

It's about a ten-minute drive from Harrison Memorial Hospital to Bremerton's ferry terminal, a ride that climbs down the hills and winds through a couple of orderly and well-maintained subdivisions before descending into the decay of Bremerton's crumbling waterfront business district. The city's tired old whore of a downtown shares its bed with any who'll have her: the state ferry terminal, the Navy Shipyard, scraggly asphalt lots full of old cars with "SPECIAL DEAL!" prices scrawled across cracked windshields. A few times a year, she rustles her tattered skirts at sailors when a Navy vessels steams in to port.

I broke the silence by asking Chester Griffin about his family.

"Two boys. Chez is thirteen—we call him that because we named him Chester Junior, and he hates being called Junior. Arthur—Art—is twelve. He's named after me too. My middle name's Arthur."

"Hmm," I said. "Proud of their namesake, I'll bet."

He looked at me like I'd just dropped a used condom in his lap. Hatred, fury, dismay. Finally, shame. The intensity of his reaction induced a trembling so severe I feared we would hit something before he pulled the car to the curb just short of the ferry terminal. He pulled a crisp handkerchief from his pocket and honked into it.

I pressed. "Our kids are what it's all about, Chester. Unless we do right by them, we're not worth a bucket of spit."

On hearing that, he looked...I don't know, different—something in his eyes at that point that I can't describe but was damned glad to see.

Sure, it was the promise of a million dollars that had gotten his attention. But it would be his view of himself as a father that would hold his commitment, and it would be his tattered but, I hoped, still redeemable code of honor and manhood that would cement it. I thought carefully about what to say next. I could not lose this man.

"Here's your chance to be a real hero, Chester. Especially to your boys." I held out my hand. "And to my boy, too." No phony imitation of John Wayne this time. Just one dad to another.

He gripped my hand tightly and didn't say anything. He just nodded. Once. Decisively. That was more than enough.

I watched Special Agent Chester Arthur Griffen drive away from the terminal and he seemed to be riding taller in the saddle. Inside the terminal, I made a quick phone call from a booth, then walked the gangplank to the Elwah, one of the more recent additions to the state's fleet.

In a few minutes we were underway, winding slowly through the narrow passage separating the Port Orchard part of the Kitsap Peninsula from the south end of Bainbridge Island. An hour later, I was in Garfield Gatsby's office in Seattle.

"What now? More murders?"

"Not yet, but the day's young." I thought about Agent Griffin, my ally, and Agent Doorham, who lay paralyzed in a Bremerton hospital. Who would be the next clay pigeon? Griffin? Me?

I told Gatsby about Griffin and Doorham. Not everything, just that Doorham might be calling him and to contact me if he did.

"That's it? That's all?"

"Oh no. There's lots more." I handed him the piece of note paper that spelled out what I wanted him to do. I had spent the entire ferry trip getting it all down on paper. Gatsby read it carefully, pursing his lips, then took off his reading glasses and rubbed the bridge of his nose.

"You can't be serious. You really want to do this? You can *afford* to do this?"

I took out my checkbook, wrote a check for fifty thousand dollars, and handed it to him. "Your retainer."

He held the check by one corner, as if it was used toilet paper. You could almost read his mind: *anyone can write a bad check.*

So I handed him the bank statement, as well.

"Oh. Well, it's your money."

"How long will it take?" I said.

His fingers tapped lightly, rhythmically, across the face of my check, as if toting beads on an abacus. Time is money. More time is more money. But too much time and I might take my shiny beads elsewhere.

"Tomorrow. I'll see the judge today and grease the skids."

"Fine. No, wait a minute…Hold off a day. Day after tomorrow."

"Whatever you say." He smiled. More time. More money.

"Yes. Day after tomorrow."

He rose from his chair as I left the office, the first time Gatsby had ever shown me that courtesy. There are millions of reasons to show respect, aren't there? All of a sudden, he had three and a half million reasons. And fifty thousand of them already in his pocket.

In the lobby of the Norton Building, I reviewed my "to do" list. Tom MacDonald was first. I used a pay phone to call him and confirmed yesterday's arrangements.

"We're still on?" He sounded a little suspicious. "I have to tell you that my editor says we need proof, not just allegations."

"Don't worry. You'll have it. Eyewitness testimony to a murder and a kidnapping. Proof enough?"

"Yeah, that would do it. Hell, yes. And, uh, you still want Nathan in on this?" He was angling for an exclusive. How often does a local newspaper reporter come out ahead of local, much less national TV?

"It's vital. This time. You'll understand, day after tomorrow. But I tell you what. I'll put it all down on paper, as if you were interviewing me, so you can run with it. I'll give that to you tomorrow, but you have to promise to hold off until after the press conference. How's that?"

That would be, he said, using an old-fashioned phrase that made him sound even more like the Clark Kent he resembled, "Swell."

"Work" was the last item on my list. I decided I could afford to blow a little more of Alice's parent's largesse, so I caught a cab to my office in Boeing's Development Center in Kent. It felt like ages since I'd last been there; it had been less than a week. I told the driver to wait for me. I wouldn't be long.

Darrell Shaeffer, the boss of our gaggle of technical writers, pulled me aside. "A guy has been calling for you a couple of times a day. Guy named Smith. Says he needs to talk to you immediately. What's up?"

I held my thumb and forefinger together to make an "O," my usual adolescent answer to that question. "Beats the hell outa me, Darrell. He leave a number?"

I already had a number for a Mr. Smith; I wondered if Darrell's Smith was my Smith. Darrell gave me the number; it matched. Darrell looked relieved when I said I would call Smith later.

"Anything else going on?" I said.

He wobbled his hand. "Same old, same old."

"Say," I said, as if the thought had just occurred to me, "Did you hear about Dan Crawford?"

Darrell's jaw hit his desk before he could retrieve it. I had asked the question only to see his reaction. Darrell had no reason to know Dan Crawford from Adam. But obviously he did. How, I wondered. Through "Smith," maybe?

He said. "Yeah. Terrible, wasn't it?"

I agreed with a nod. *Et tu*, Darrell?

Before I left, I stopped at my desk and called Smith. I wasn't surprised to hear he wanted to see me, soon. Tomorrow, if possible. "Are you available for lunch?" he asked. "Metropolitan Grill at Second and Marion?"

I agreed to meet him, then called home. Agent Chester Arthur Griffin answered the phone, conveying a great deal of warmth in just a few words. There had been no additional calls, he said, and no, Em and Alice weren't home yet, and yes, he would be happy to meet my 3:45 ferry. David Welch, the Bainbridge cop, would man the phone.

The ferry ride across the sound reminded me that there are few better places to spend 35 minutes. I drank my brew on the top deck, like everyone else, disregarding the admonition posted in the cafeteria: "State Law requires that all alcoholic beverage be consumed in the dining area." I drank my beer and counted other peoples' sailboats. A hundred and twenty-four. My personal best.

Griffin met the boat and we got home just in time for me to sign for a shipment from UPS. Both Griffin and Welch checked the package carefully, Griffin actually sniffing it at one point. They pronounced it safe; it wasn't a bomb, in their considered opinion. I slit the twine on the brick-sized package, noting there was no return address. I also noted that both of them had backed away from the counter as I removed the wrapping.

Inside the brown paper was a cardboard box full of peanut-shaped bits of Styrofoam surrounding a small plastic zip-top bag. Mindful of the need to preserve any fingerprints, I picked up the bag by a corner and flicked away a couple of clinging Styrofoam peanuts.

The bag was cold to the touch, its interior fogged over, its cargo not quite visible. I unzipped the top of the bag and tipped the contents onto the kitchen counter.

A steaming piece of dry ice rolled out, skittered across the counter, and fell to the floor, followed by another small object, pebble-grained and frosty grayish pink in color, raised veins of dark blue tracing its surface—an egg-shaped marble that wobbled to a stop at the edge of the counter.

After a few seconds, my brain registered what I was seeing: a very frigid testicle.

14

Because he had once been in the enemy camp and because he had a sickly look of guilt on his face, but mostly because he was within reach, I turned on agent Griffin. My round-house right pin-wheeled him across the dining room and through the screen door occupying the space that also used to hold a sliding glass door. Griffin landed on his hands and knees on the deck. I hurried outside to apologize.

"No need. That's all right. I deserved that." He brushed pieces of torn screen aside as he picked himself up and rubbed his chin. "Oh, I meant to tell you, Lumberman's is sending a new slider out tomorrow, along with an installer. I put it on the FBI's Amex card. The least I could do. I'll make sure they install a new screen too." He grinned.

We went back inside. Griffin poked the frozen testicle back into the plastic bag and instructed officer Welch to take it to the Seattle PD for analysis in their lab. Not to the FBI lab for analysis, I noted. I hoped to God it would turn out to be canine in origin—from the dog Rick saw mutilated by the kidnappers. Let it be a mutt's nut, I prayed. Not Rick's, Miguel's, or DJ's.

Em and Alice arrived home just as Welch left. I greeted them in the parking lot, and they were as anxious to bring me up to date as I was to keep them in the dark about the surprise package I had just received. So they did, and I did, as my mind tried to shrug off the awful image of the primal fear of the male of the species.

Their meeting with the editor of the *Post Intelligencer* had gone well, as had their meeting with Dale Kennedy, our favorite printer. Dale is an unreconstructed hippie who operates an "alternative" print shop, the only one in the country, he claims. Which means you have to persuade him to print what you want him to print, because he will print only what he deems worthy of the trees that sacrificed their lives. Or you can go to another printer with more flexible values. Inasmuch as Bainbridge Island is ecologically greener than any other Emerald Isle, Dale has more customers than he can beat off with a pail of soy-based ink.

So far, everything was going according to plan. The *PI* editor had been agreeable. Dale had been enthusiastic. Agent Griffin was cooperating. We offered our congratulations to each other, while I strove to blot out the memory of a nodule of frozen flesh wobbling across the kitchen counter.

"What's the matter, honey? You look like you've seen a ghost." Em didn't miss anything.

"Oh, just a little nervous, I guess. Almost feels like this is going too easily," I said a little louder than normal as we entered the house. I hoped Agent Griffin would get the message to keep his mouth closed.

Agent Griffin gave the women a small hug and me a small nod that told me he would keep our little secret. I let my breath out slowly

Eventually we all got hungry, but I didn't feel like dining at our kitchen counter. So Em, Alice, and I piled into Alice's Blazer and headed for Mommie Dearest's house, intending to take Jane with us to dinner somewhere. We knew Jane's kids were staying with her in-laws, up in Sequim.

Jane had a better idea. "Let's dine together: all of us, my kids, and Gladys and Bill." She made a quick phone call and we headed toward the Olympic Peninsula.

Sequim's an oddball place, climate-wise, out of synch with the rest of western part of the Pacific Northwest. The northern hemisphere's only true temperate rain forest, the Hoh Rain Forest, is but a hundred miles west of Sequim, across the Olympic Range. There, the moisture-laden low-pressure weather systems of the north Pacific expel a dozen-plus feet of rain a year as they roll up the western slopes of the Olympics.

Nearby Sequim, on the other hand, sits in a narrow rain-shadow valley just east of those Olympic peaks; by the time the clouds reach the valley they've been wrung dry, and Sequim's precipitation mirrors that of the Sonora Desert. Golf courses need irrigation and sunny days far outnumber cloudy ones in this solarium of the Pacific Northwest.

Not just damp Seattleites, but retirees from all over the country have flocked to the area in recent years, among them the late Dan Crawford's parents, Gladys and Wild Bill.

As we rode along, we told Jane what we had been doing, especially the good news about Agent Chester Griffin becoming our as-yet unannounced ace in the hole.

At Sequim, we turned toward the water—the Straits of Juan de Fuca—and drove directly to Gladys and Wild Bill's five-acre mini-ranch. Gladys, Bill, and Jane's kids were waiting with Bill and Gladys next to their old Buick, a hamper of food and six packs of beer and soda already in its trunk. We headed off, Wild Bill leading the way.

For the next two hours, we tried to forget our troubles with a good old-fashioned picnic at the beach. The kids collected buckets of shells and dozens of pieces of unusual driftwood, and we all collected plenty of Vitamin D from the sun's rays. Before we headed back to Sequim, I took Wild Bill aside and filled him in too. He gave me that long, hard stare that looks authentic only on high-plains ranchers and Clint Eastwood. Bill's weather-beaten face had been doing a fine job of masking the emotion he must have been feeling at the violent death of his only son and the kidnapping of his favorite grandson.

"Thanks for tellin' me, Andy. Just couldn't make no sense of it, no damn sense a'tall." He rubbed the scrabble on his chin. "Think we'll get em? Bastards what got Dan 'n our boys?" The Montanan's dam burst then, salty runnels filling the crevasses of his face. He didn't bother to wipe the tears away. I don't think he was even aware of them until he saw them mirrored on my face. Then he swatted at them as if they were pesky horse flies.

"We gotta get those sons-a-bitches, Andy. We gotta."

"We will, Bill. I promise."

"When ya need another hand, lemme know. I'm a crack shot with any gun ya care t' name, 'n' I'd be more 'n' happy t' help ya blow 'em away."

I didn't doubt it for a minute. "Are you going to say anything to Gladys?"

"'Bout your plan? Naw. Don't think so. Old gal's got a finicky ticker, ya know. Later maybe, when it's over—when we get our boys back. Yeah, then I'll tell her." He looked out to sea. "But I am gonna tell Dan's kids. They got a right t' know 'bout their dad 'n' why he died. Tain't nothin' wrong with their tickers. Mine neither." He thumped his chest, a sound like a kettle drum, or a keg half full of dynamite.

Just before we left Bill and Gladys' place at eleven o'clock, I called home. There had been no messages from the kidnappers, nor any—through Garfield Gatsby—from Agent Griffin's colleague, Doorham.

"Guess we can rule out George's help, huh?" Chester Griffin said. "But, hey, there's some good news too, really good news. That testicle was from a dog. It wasn't human. Thought you'd be glad to know that."

"Thank God."

"Are you still in Sequim with Mizz Crawford's folks?"

I told him we were and that Jane Crawford would be staying behind with her kids and her inlaws, but Em, Alice, and I were just about to head back. He seemed pleased. He had given officer Welch the night off to spend with his family, and was happy I'd called. Then he needed to say something more.

"You don't have to be in a hurry to get home, Andy. Everything is under control here. This case is going to blow wide open pretty soon. We're going to put the whole lot of them away, all of 'em, once and for all. We'll get your boys back too. If it's the last thing I do, I'll make sure of that."

With allies as staunch as Chester Griffin and Wild Bill Crawford, I didn't doubt it. I thanked Griffin and asked him to leave the outside lights on. "Don't wait up," I said. "We'll be late, I'm sure."

It was nearly 11:30 before we turned onto Highway 101, heading back toward the Hood Canal Bridge, the Kitsap Peninsula, then across the Agate Pass bridge to Bainbridge Island. Home.

We arrived late, nicely exhausted. It had been a great day for our side. We had stopped briefly for pie at the Sands in Poulsbo, but were too weary to make sensible conversation, so we pressed on toward the island. Our day had been full, and we had done everything we could to get ready for the kidnappers' call tomorrow—only a few hours from now, if they kept their word. We were tired, but eager to see everything play out to the happy conclusion we hoped was very near. Fingers crossed, tomorrow our nightmare would end.

Make that today, I remember thinking as I glanced at the dashboard clock as we headed down Gertie Johnson Road, the one-lane driveway that wound down the hillside to the parking lot just north of our house on the boardwalk. It was exactly 3:30 a.m. Whew. We *had* made a day of it. Knowing the hour made me even more tired, even more happy to be home.

105

I didn't sound the horn as I usually did before steering down the narrow drive. No need to worry about encountering oncoming traffic this time of night, no reason to disturb the neighbors.

As we approached the parking area, we could see that Chester had left lots of light on, both inside and outside the house. A nice sight: our home: pretty, friendly and welcoming.

In a flash, a whooshing roar shook the car, and a blinding yellow fireball shot a hundred feet skyward. Pieces of our house, our deck, and Special Agent Chester Arthur Griffin followed the flames high into the shattered night.

On the other side of the island—at precisely the same instant, as near as could be determined later—the Crawford house, mooring dock, sailboat, and Chris-Craft cruiser were scattered across a tidal inlet by similar explosions.

Bainbridge Police Officer David Welch, who had been sent home by Agent Griffin but felt far too keyed up to relax, decided instead to make an impromptu tour of the island he loved to serve and protect. His police cruiser was directly opposite the Crawford house at its moment of detonation and he was impaled by a four-by-four post that speared the driver's door. He died on the operating table two hours later.

Two houses down the walk from our house, Harold Kluender, a retired bachelor plumber of randy renown, died within moments of the explosion. The official cause of death was cardiac arrest. Atypically, he had been in bed alone.

Our immediate neighbors, Albert and Sandy Bass, scarred veterans of twelve years of marital war, had gone to their adjoining twin beds following their usual bed-time skirmish. Jostled to the floor between their beds, they were more confused than damaged by the next-door blast. Nine months after their sundered early morning, following the birth of their first child, they would praise God's intervention in saving their marriage as well as their lives.

The Cwazy Wabbit, parked next to the house, was a goner, the explosion of its gas tank a slightly delayed echo of the blast that converted our dream-house to a waterfront black hole.

I suppose we were in shock. We didn't—couldn't—move from the Blazer until the first fire truck arrived. Idiotically, I looked at the dashboard again, as if it mattered how quickly firefighters could cool the dying embers. Seven minutes. Not bad for a mostly volunteer fire department, I remember thinking.

Some of the firefighters trained their hoses on the Kluender and Bass homes, while others made sure that Sandy and Albert Bass were safe, then discovered Clarence Kluender's body. The furnishings of both houses ended up thoroughly saturated, but both houses were saved.

By dawn's early light, there was enough left of our house to fill the bed of a small pickup. Only the fireplace and part of the masonry chimney remained partly intact, flipping Seattle a broken, blackened bird. Someone found Agent Griffin's head shortly after dawn, in the back yard of the house atop the cliff behind our house. Bits and pieces of our prize witness would be retrieved throughout the day, some floating just offshore. Judging by the size of the small lump in the black body bag, half a kitchen trash bag would have sufficed.

By seven, the arson and bomb squads of the Seattle Police had arrived, along with large contingents of FBI and ATF specialists. After poking and sifting our rubble and the Crawfords', they concluded that plastique-type explosives had been used, detonated by radio-controlled transmitters. Those devices were sophisticated, they said, available only to the U.S. military and well-trusted allies. And, we figured, certain three-lettered agencies of the U.S. government.

By eleven o'clock, Em, Alice, and I had repeated our accounts of what we witnessed so many times, to so many people, that jurisdiction of our "case" was as up in the air as the scorched molecules of our former home. The FBI insisted on overall jurisdiction because everything seemed to stem from the original kidnapping. The ATF predicated their claim for investigative primacy on the use of explosives. The Seattle police argued the overriding aspects of murder and arson. Bainbridge Island's Police Department and firefighters, the Port Angeles PD, and the Clallam County Sheriff's office just shook their heads, content to abdicate to any of their larger, louder siblings.

As for me, I didn't give a damn. As far as I could see, I knew more than anyone else knew, and I was a hell of a lot more motivated than anyone. The only people I trusted at the moment were Em, Alice, and Wild Bill Crawford. Less than twelve hours ago, that short list had included Special Agent Chester Arthur Griffin.

Em finally realized that, thanks to all the bureaucratic bickering, no one had thought about reconnecting our disrupted phone line, or those at the Crawfords', so the kidnappers could call as planned. When she suggested such a course of action to the Seattle police, they arranged to have Qwest reroute both lines to their headquarters in Seattle. The FBI man, miffed at being outflanked, complained to me. Not to Em, to me. Figured. The sexist pig.

My stare sent him away. He mumbled something about checking with Washington. The other Washington, I presumed.

Finally, we were allowed to leave. Exhausted but far too keyed up to sleep, we headed automatically to Pegasus Coffee in Winslow, unconsciously seeking comfort in the known and familiar. We had the place to ourselves. Everyone else, even Jonathan, who normally worked until the afternoon rush began at 3:00, was out gaping at exploded houses and docks. Just Jack, Pegasus's owner, was around, and he was busy unloading a produce truck.

"Boy, am I glad to see you guys are okay! Help yourself to coffee and I'll get some pastries out as soon as I stow this food."

We sat in the front booth with our coffee and tried regroup. Our case appeared to be blown to bits. Without Griffin's testimony incriminating the FBI, no one could tie the FBI and Boeing to the killing of Dan Crawford and the kidnapping of our boys. For that matter, without the missing microfiches, we had no proof that Dan himself was ever even involved. Worse, we felt such a personal sense of loss, not so much because our house was gone, but because Dan and now, Agent Griffin, had died in vain. No one could do anything for either one of them now, except their God, and His or Her sense of fairness. I had to feel that Dan's attempts to "go straight" and to safeguard his family, however unsuccessful they'd been, had to count for something. For sure Griffin's final acts of atonement had produced absolution for his earlier wrongdoing.

But God did not appear to be on our side. What the bloody hell did he expect us to do now?

Eventually we concluded we had only two options. We could Continue on our present course, or we could do nothing. But we could not, would not, do nothing.

Our only choice was to press onward. Shattered as our plan was, it was the only plan we had. If we were to have any hope of getting our boys back, we would have to bluff our way through, as if we already had all the evidence we needed.

So that's what we would do. Em and Alice would borrow a car from Brad, a friend who owned a car repair business. He always had an extra junker or three in his yard. Em called Brad, and Brad offered to deliver a "pretty decent" Pontiac immediately. While Brad was headed to Pegasus, I used Pegasus's phone to call Mister Smith and postpone our lunch date.

Then I took the Alice's Blazer and drove to Bremerton. In 30 minutes, I was at Agent Doorham's bedside, making him an offer he couldn't refuse.

15

Doorham's fight-or-flight impulse short-circuited from trying to do both at the same time. Shocked to see me alive, I'm sure he wished that his Glock was in easy reach—and that could control some part of his body below his neck long enough to reach it. But it wasn't, and he couldn't. Nor could he run away; but his eyes, darting about seeking an exit, hadn't gotten the message.

His mouth still worked, but that moment he wasn't having much luck calling for help. My hands tightened slowly, deliciously, around his throat. I felt the cartilage of his voice box flexing inward like the trampled hose of a vacuum cleaner. In a few seconds the ridges of that cleverly designed protective structure would snap and crunch his voice into a permanent croak that would make Kermit the Frog sound manly, even to Miss Piggy. As delightful as that prospect seemed, I needed a different result so eased up a bit. I whispered in his ear, not wanting to alert anyone monitoring the intercom.

"Listen up, dickface. You have ninety excruciatingly painful seconds to live. Your colleague, a better Special Agent than you've ever been—and a Bainbridge cop who was one of the best men anyone will ever know—were blown to bits this morning. That's no surprise to you, of course. You know that already. But guess what? Your asshole buddies missed me." I squeezed a bit harder. "And now it's your turn. But because I'm such a decent man, I'll give you a choice. I ought to kill you right now—actually, in about seventy seconds, because that's how long it will take for you to asphyxiate. But I'll give you a chance to extend that a bit—long enough to talk to the cops. Real cops. Then the King County Prosecuting Attorney."

I squeezed harder still. "So. You wanna die or you wanna talk? Makes no difference to me, asshole. You're gone either way."

His eyes bulged. I kept increasing the pressure. I got so enthralled watching his eyes bug out that I almost missed seeing his tongue wagging up and down. I gave his neck one more hard squeeze before letting go.

He inhaled hoarsely through the fish bones stuck in his throat. "I'll talk," He croaked, coughing a spatter of blood onto the sheet tucked under his immobile, folded arms. He swallowed once, grimacing. Damn. He would live.

The duty nurse slammed into the room on the run.

"What's wrong? I heard this awful croaking sound."

"Agent Doorham had a frog in his throat. He was trying to tell me to have you call the police immediately. He said he wants to confess his role in three murders and in kidnapping three children."

The nurse looked at me like I had wandered over from the psycho ward. Then she looked at Doorham, who hesitated, then finally nodded his concurrence.

"*Now*, nurse, if you don't mind," I said. "Make the call." She left the room. Thirty seconds later an orderly preceded her return.

"What's going on?" the orderly said.

"The nurse didn't tell you?"

"Yeah, but…"

"Did you call the police, nurse?"

"Yes, but…"

"And you brought this good fellow along to watch the killer until the police get here. Good thinking. Given what he knows and the folks he will be implicating, lots of people are going to want to shut him up."

Doorham remained as silent as the Sphinx. He would talk, but only to the police. I couldn't be certain what he would say.

"You sure, now, Doorham? I won't leave you alone here until you confirm to these good people that you want to confess your part in killing Dan Crawford, FBI Agent Griffin, and Officer David Welch. And in kidnapping three teen-age boys: Dan Crawford Junior, Miguel Sharp, and my son, Rick Eastman. So speak up."

He looked me straight in the eye. I could see he knew that *my* commitment hadn't faltered, that I would find a way to kill him if he didn't confess.

"Yes." That was to me. Then he looked at the nurse and the orderly. "Yes, he's right. I need to talk to the police right away, to tell them about…what he said. What I did." His voice sounded almost normal.

"Well, no sense me waiting around here, then. The cops will be here shortly. Nurse, remind them to inform the Seattle Police, too. And above all, don't let anyone into this room until the police arrive. Agent Doorham's colleague has already been murdered and someone might try to get to Agent Doorham too, before the police arrive—or afterwards."

Someone as dangerous as an angry father, say.

I didn't really want to leave Doorman alone to speak to the police, but time was tight and I couldn't wait. I had very little time to get the rest of the plan in place. Back at the nurses' station, I got permission from the same nurse to use her phone to call Garfield Gatsby. While I waited for his secretary to connect us, the nurse handed me a cup of coffee from her personal pot. I nodded my thanks.

"Change of plans," I told Gatsby when he came on the line. "Serve those papers today. Within the hour. Any problems with that?"

He allowed as how he could handle it.

"One more thing," I said. "There are two more plaintiffs, the estates of Special Agent Chester Arthur Griffin and Bainbridge Police Officer David Welch."

"Why?"

"Because they're dead. And because I owe them, big time."

"You do realize there will be extra costs associated with simultaneous service of so many defendants in so many locations, don't you?"

"Does that bother you?"

"No, but…"

"Just do it. And one more thing. My wife will be delivering a plain-language summary of the suit. It should be coming off the press just about now, if my guess is right. Give that summary to the *Times* and *PI* people right away, as soon as they arrive at your office. Is that clear?"

It was.

"The reporters will be in your office at two o'clock. But don't give them the summary until you are certain that all of the defendants have been served."

"Yes, of course. I understand."

Then I placed another call, this one to the seventeenth floor of the Federal Building. I was put through to the acting head of the U.S. Coast Guard detachment, Captain Billingsley.

"I was wondering if you would be calling. I saw the news this morning. I'm terribly sorry."

I thanked him for his concern, and he responded by anticipating the purpose of my call.

"I do have that information you asked for about Commander Bottoms. Will you be stopping by to pick it up? It does show the connection you mentioned."

"No, just have someone hand-carry it across the street to the Norton Building, if you would." I gave him Gatsby's name and office location.

"No problem. I'll deliver it to Gatsby myself, right now."

I rang off and started dialing another number. "This one's long-distance," I said to the nurse. But it's really important. Can I do that?"

She smiled. "Hang up and start over. Dial nine, then eight, then one, then the number, including area code."

Wild Bill Crawford answered his phone in Sequim with a vengeance, like he had been camped on it, daring the kidnappers to call. He had heard about the island demolition derby already; the Bainbridge PD had notified Jane immediately after the explosion. I think Wild Bill was a little disappointed that it was only me calling, not the creeps who had his grandson, but he listened carefully, especially when I told him that I might need his help soon.

"I'll look forward t' that, son. You know how t' get aholt a me."

It was almost one o'clock now, and I still had three more calls to make. The first was to Mr. Smith at Boeing, to confirm our lunch plans.

"Certainly. We're still on."

"Good. I'll meet you in the bar at the Metropolitan. Find a table where we can see the television." He seemed puzzled but agreed.

The next call was pure pleasure, to Darrell Schaeffer, my boss at Boeing.

"I quit, Darrell."

"Huh? Quit?! How come, Andy?"

"You'll find out soon enough. Read this evening's *Times* or watch the news. Oh...and Darrell?"

"Yeah?"

"You bet on the wrong team, buddy. And I'm holding your marker, so guard your kneecaps."

My last call was to the Seattle Police. They had no new information. I told them to call the Bremerton hospital and the Bremerton PD for a hot scoop.

I thanked the nurse profusely, fled down the stairs to Alice's Blazer, sped to the terminal, and skidded aboard the 1:00 Bremerton ferry just before it left for Seattle.

16

At 2:30, I walked into the bar at the Metropolitan Grill. I'd kept Smith waiting, but it didn't matter; his attention and that of the twenty or thirty other late lunch-drinkers was riveted on the 40-inch screen behind the bar. Smith was easy to spot in the crowd; his was not the only executive's face watching the screen, but it was the only one with that precise gray-white coloring and such an uneasy look about the eyes. I slid onto a stool at the end of the bar where I could monitor the broadcast and keep an eye on Smith, too.

The screen showed reporters and photographers for Channels 4, 5, 7, 11, and 13 and the *Seattle Times, Seattle Post Intelligencer,* all jammed up in the tastefully gray reception area of Gatsby, McClain, and McGinty. Garfield Gatsby, looking rather gray and pasty himself, was striving to maintain a dignified air.

An announcer's voice-over summarized events as they had unfolded so far. A suit had been filed against The Boeing Company, the Federal Bureau of Investigation, the Department of Defense, and several named individuals in each organization, including the Chairman of the Board for The Boeing Company, the Chiefs of Staff of the Army, Navy, Air Force and Marine Corps, and the Secretaries of the Army, Navy, and Air Force.

The scene on the screen reprised footage from early morning news broadcasts: smoldering ruins of the Crawfords' house and ours. The narrator told of the deaths of the FBI's Special Agent Griffin and the Bainbridge PD's Officer Welch. My name was mentioned three times, as the father of one of the kidnapped boys, owner of one of the smoldering ruins, and lead plaintiff in the lawsuit.

A quick cut to Seattle's local FBI office showed a live reporter button-holing some poor guy holding the fort. The reporter read him the section of our plain-language summary of the suit accusing the Bureau of master-minding the kidnapping of Daniel Crawford Junior, Miguel Sharp, and Rick Eastman, as well as the murders of Daniel Crawford Senior and FBI agent Chester Arthur Griffin.

"Preposterous. The Bureau fights crime; it doesn't commit it." His response would have been more effective if he hadn't been backpedaling toward an inner office.

Next, a helicopter view of Boeing's skyscraper in Chicago, followed by file footage of its CEO addressing the Seattle Chamber of Commerce before he moved the company's corporate office to the windy city, and another of him accepting a federal quality improvement award presented by the Secretary of Defense and the Administrator of NASA. This morning, Boeing had allowed no cameras into its new corporate high-rise building at 100 North Riverside Plaza, and so far had refused all requests for information.

A network feed elaborated the full cast of bad guys. There was a view of the U.S. Capitol Building, then the J. Edgar Hoover Building, then an unnamed spokeswoman for the FBI, also refusing comment "...until we have reviewed the allegations in the suit itself." Additional spokespersons for the accused four-starred Pentagon co-conspirators similarly dissembled. Finally, the president's press secretary was shown reading a statement promising "...a complete investigation by the Justice Department, with a full report as soon as possible."

The final 30-second wrap-up by an atypically sober airhead at Seattle's CBS affiliate concluded with the traditional "We now return you to our normal programming." Ominous organ music for a soap opera filled the air. The bartender grimaced, pointed a remote at the TV and reduced its volume, then switched the channel to ESPN.

I have to confess to being a little miffed that I had received so little personal coverage—far less than my 15-minute entitlement. Ah, well, there was something to be said for anonymity. I walked over to Smith's table and sat down across from him. He looked up at me. He appeared ill. Ah, finally. Recognition.

"How much?" I said.

"What?"

"How much are you going to offer me to call off the press?"

"Huh?"

"Isn't that why we're meeting?"

"No. Of course not."

"Okay. We'll play it your way. What *did* you want to see me about?"

Some seconds passed. He wiped a slick of oily perspiration from his upper lip and forehead, using a napkin I had watched him use several times in the newscast.

"Whenever you're ready, Mister Smith."

"I was asked to talk to you to see if you would be interested in helping us at Boeing, as an employee…"

"Ex-employee. I quit today."

"Yes, that's right. So I've been informed. Former employee, then." Word traveled quickly. My old boss must have reported my dereliction immediately. Thanks, Darrell.

"So what were you going to offer me? Dan Crawford's old job?" Smith looked disgusted at the mention of Dan. "You remember. The guy mentioned on TV. Used to collect debts for Boeing. He's collecting mold in the morgue now. That Dan Crawford."

"I see you are not ready to help us." Smith started to rise, looking both angry and frustrated. "I see you are part of the problem, not part of the solution. If you'll excuse me…."

"Sit down, Mister Smith. Otherwise I might feel compelled to identify myself—and you—to these good people."

Smith sat down. His forehead had produced a fresh sheen of sweat. He needed another martini, so he could get a fresh napkin. I ordered one for him and a Red Hook ale for myself.

When our drinks arrived, Smith downed his in a few rapid swallows. He seemed a little more in control. My God, the way he was behaving, you'd think *I* was in the wrong.

I said, "Was it you who fingered Dan Crawford?" He looked disgusted.

"Never mind," I said. "Trick question. You've probably stopped beating your wife, too."

"Okay, let's play this your way. What exactly do you want, Mister Eastman?" There was resignation in his voice, like he was as sick of everything as I was.

"I want you to carry a message back to Boeing and to Boeing's partners in this whole affair. Tell them…"

I found myself actually steepling my fingers in anticipation. "Tell them I can't be bought, at any price. I *will* win my suit and I *will* get my share of the hundred and fifty million we've asked for in damages. My share of that, plus the satisfaction of seeing all of you sent to prison, will be more than adequate compensation."

"You honestly think you will win." His incredulity seemed genuine. Maybe his legal training was coming back to him: never go on the defensive, always attack.

"Of course. We have the sworn testimony of an FBI agent, and now you have every investigative reporter in the country looking over your shoulder. Their pickings have been a little slim lately. Not much for them since Watergate, Iran-Contra-gate, Whitewater-gate, and Monica's blue dress. They will be all over you guys like flies on a pile of dead lawyers. You can convey another message, too."

"Yes?"

"The most important one of all: Dan Crawford Junior, Miguel Sharp, and my son must be returned to us immediately, unharmed. And I mean right away. Right now.

"You can also tell whomever you report to that I *do* know about the information that Dan Crawford had before he was killed, and I *will* soon have it in my possession. I'm sure you all wish he'd flushed it down the toilet, but he didn't…"

"What information?"

"Can it, Smith. We both know what we are talking about…"

My voice trailed off, despite my anger. I'd been bluffing, of course, but now a part of my mind was trying to supply me with something that would turn my bluff into reality, if I would just shut up and listen to it. It was so close that I could almost taste it. Something I'd just said—about the hiding place of Dan's microfiches and a flushing toilet. Bells were dinging, loudly. But it was just indiscriminate clanging.

"You look like you were remembering where something was hidden," Smith said. "So, now who's holding back on who?"

"Whom," I said. The correction was automatic.

"Forget it," I continued. "I'm not about to reveal the exact content of that information to your crew, much less where it's located. They'll find out soon enough. Tell them that."

Except I didn't know—but I *did* know something, if my brain would just connect the dots. What was it?

"Yes." Smith's eyes narrowed as he rose to leave, once more the senior executive in charge, the lawyer in full possession of his faculties.

"Yes," he said. "I'll make my report. You may be certain we will be in touch."

I didn't doubt it. Why did I suddenly feel so uneasy?

17

In all the time the Washington State Ferry System has operated boats on Puget Sound, I don't suppose many passengers had been paged for an incoming shore-to-ship phone call. The announcement came over the boat's intercom just as the boat was preparing to leave Colman Dock, asking me to go to the Second Mate's cabin on the north side of the boat. So I took my coffee to the Second Mate's cabin, leaned across the top half of the open Dutch door, and identified myself.

"Come on in. Call for you on that phone," she said, flicking her hand toward the phone on her desk, then returning to her perusal of an employee newsletter. I set my coffee on her desk and picked up the phone. She picked up my coffee.

"Thanks," she said, taking a big sip. "Nice and hot. Cream too, just as I like it."

"Andy Eastman," I said into the receiver, a smile on my face.

"Sergeant Russo, Seattle Police, Mister Eastman. Glad we caught you before the boat left. We need you here at the station right away."

"What's up?"

"We'll talk about that when you get here. A car will be waiting for you in front of the terminal."

"Can't you tell me over the phone?"

"I'll see you in just a few minutes, Mister Eastman," Sergeant Russo said.

"Wait a minute. I've got a car on board."

"I'll have someone drive it off the other end. Give your keys to a crew member."

The Second Mate held out her hand. "Keys to your car?" Apparently she'd taken the call in the first place. I handed them over. "What are you driving and where did you park?" she asked, and I told her. "Go to the Bainbridge PD when you get back," she said. "Your car will be there."

As I left, she thanked me for the coffee.

The cop car was in front of the ferry terminal as promised, and the driver, a black guy in plain clothes who favored the pastel undercover Miami Vice look, could tell me nothing—said he couldn't, anyway. He was just the driver dispatched by Sergeant Russo.

He got us to the police building on Fourth Avenue before I remembered to fasten my seatbelt, and ushered me to Russo's office, a tiny glass-enclosed office in a large room full of battered desks occupied by officers drinking from mugs caked with so much coffee drool you couldn't read their captions. A fax machine stuttered away in a corner, next to a muttering computer printer. All over the room, phones rang; no one seemed in a hurry to answer them.

Russo shook my hand and closed the door to his office, shutting out some of the noise.

"Have a seat please, Mister Eastman."

He was ill at ease. My stomach clenched. I took a deep breath and let it out slowly. "What is it?"

Russo reached toward a small recorder on his desk. "I'm very sorry, but you need to listen to this. Brace yourself. It's not pleasant."

He pressed the button on the recorder and I steeled myself to hear my son's voice again. Instead a scream leaped out of the recorder, careened off the glass walls of the cubicle, and bored into my brain like a kamikaze earwig. My hands clapped my ears by instinct. Too late. Much too late.

Russo pulled my arms down, gently. "Was that your son's voice, do you think?" I shook my head back and forth. The scream didn't sound like Rick. Maybe Dan Junior. Or Miguel. I couldn't be sure.

"That came in on your line a little while ago. Just that, nothing else. We think it's from the kidnappers."

"When? When did it come in?"

"Two-thirty-five."

"Oh, Jesus," I said. "During the newscast. Has Mommie Dearest, I mean, Jane Crawford, heard this?"

121

"Sequim PD just sent someone to her with a copy of the tape."

"I don't think it's Rick, my son…I'm pretty sure it's not Rick…."

"Okay."

"I hope to God it's not Rick…."

"I understand."

"I hope it's not anyone…I hope it's a fake…."

"We do, too, Mister Eastman. But we have to assume it's genuine."

"I suppose so. I, uh, is there anything else? Can I go now?" I had to get away from there right now, or I'd be puking on his desk.

"Yes, of course, of course. Thank you for coming in. Please let us know where you will be staying tonight, won't you? In case we need to get in touch?"

"The Captain's House," I mumbled.

"The Captain's House. A bed and breakfast on Bainbridge?"

"Yeah. Up the street from Pegasus Coffee, near the marina. A friend owns it. I don't know the phone number."

"We'll get it." Russo got up from his desk and came around to help me to my feet. My muscle control was minimal. All my brain cells were tuned to a God-awful scream in my head, echoing atonally. Russo kept hold of my right hand and I finally realized attempting he was trying to say something.

"I think you are being quite a brave man, Mister Eastman. It takes guts to take on Boeing, the Department of Defense *and* the FBI."

I heard him but I couldn't respond. I could only return his gaze. I was grateful for the compliment but he didn't understand anything. Guts had nothing to do with it. It was the survival of my son. Didn't he get that? I didn't have the strength to try to explain.

"Thank you," I said.

"Let's hope it works. Let's hope they let them go."

Once again, I was wrong. Russo did understand.

The same cop returned me to the ferry terminal, where I waited for fifteen minutes until the next boat came in. I sat on a wounded knife-scarred bench in a room filling up with commuters leaving for home early. I'm sure it was noisy, but to me it was as silent as a tomb, compared to the screams in my head.

18

I got to the Captain's House at four-thirty. The front door was un-locked, but the B&B's owner, Marilyn Hensel, wasn't home. Marilyn worked during the day as a child psychologist for the Seattle school system. During the summer, her slowest time as a psychologist but busiest season at the B&B, she manned her office only two days a week. This was one of those days. I found a note from Em and Alice on the kitchen counter. They were at Pegasus.

Leaving Alice's blazer parked in Marilyn's driveway, I walked the half-block to the coffee shop. I didn't spot them; except for Jack, the place was empty. He said he thought the girls were out on the pier, getting some sun.

"Andy?" he said.

"Yeah?"

"I'm so sorry about Rick. About your house, too. About every-thing. Terrible thing. And you think Boeing and the FBI and all are in on it?"

"I know they are."

"Damn. Drive those bastards into the sea and drown 'em, Andy. And if you need any help, you let me know."

His vehemence startled me. Jack was a died-in-the-wool pacifist who rarely offered opinions stronger than his coffee. Come to think of it, that allowed him considerable latitude.

"Thanks, Jack. We're going to do just that."

"Any help at all. Just let me know. I mean it."

I walked out the side door and headed past the Chandlery building toward the entrance gate of the marina. Em and Alice were sitting on a low wooden curb alongside the gate. They stood as they saw me coming and gave me simultaneous hugs that squeezed out some tears, tears I'd managed to avoid shedding when I'd first heard that recorded scream. Now they spilled out and I couldn't stop them. I turned toward Pegasus so Em and Alice wouldn't see them.

"Let's get some coffee," I said, unable to hide the catch in my throat. I needed to tell them about the call without shattering their hopes as badly as mine had been. But I needed the crutch of a cup of coffee to get through my story. Then I needed a cigarette too, and lighted one without thinking. Pegasus is very much a no-smoking place, like most places these days. Jack didn't say anything as he came over and sat with us. Just one other table was occupied, by a young couple I didn't recognize, who were conversing softly but intensely at a table in the back corner.

When the couple noticed me smoking, they headed for the front door quickly, giving me the kind of look we smokers are used to seeing, a combination of pity and a wish we'd just self-immolate.

Jack said to them, "Thanks, folks. No need to hurry back." He tapped me on the arm. "Got another?" I handed him a Camel.

"I didn't know you smoked, Jack. Especially here."

"I smoke when I want to. Someone gonna throw me out of my own place?"

Em knew something was up. The redness in my eyes and the catch in my voice had given me away. "Your meeting with Smith didn't go well?"

I stubbed out my cigarette in the last dregs of coffee in my cup and took Em's hands in mine. "No darling. It's not Smith." I hesitated.

Alice too must have sensed something awful coming. She reached out and put her hands on top of ours. I wished I didn't have to, but I told them about the latest call from the kidnappers and watched their faces turn white.

"But I don't think it was either Rick or Miguel," I added quickly. "It sounded more like Dan Junior. I can't be certain, but I think it was DJ." And damn me all to hell, I needed it to be Dan Junior and not Rick or Miguel. Especially not Rick. "I'm pretty sure it was DJ who was screaming."

"Let's hope so," said Alice. She looked up at me. "Sorry, that's an awful thing to say, but I can't help it."

"Got another of those?" Em asked.

"You sure?"

"God, yes. Gimme a cigarette." I lighted it and handed it to her, just like I used to before she quit.

"Me, too," said Alice. So I lighted one for her, and another for myself. And finally, I fired up one for Jack and handed it to him.

"Thanks, honey," he said.

Without our laughter just then, we'd have flipped out completely. Jack excused himself for a moment, then returned with a pot of coffee and a plate of sugar-dusted cake donuts still warm from the fryer.

"On the house, guys," he said, setting everything on the coffee table. He flipped the sign on the door to "closed," then left us alone.

We gobbled the donuts and finished that pot of coffee and another while rehashing all that had happened during the day. My visit with Agent Doorham and Doorham's agreement to tell the truth. My meeting with Smith. Em and Alice's meetings with Gatsby and *Times* and *PI* people. Their subsequent spontaneous visits to the widows of FBI Agent Chester Griffin, Bainbridge Officer David Welch, and Coast Guard Commander Bottoms.

Ingesting all that coffee and all those donuts and all that information—and yes, eating all that smoke—helped us feel better, maybe even a little high from the combination. We had done what we could, everything we could think of, anyway. We knew the press was on our side, and now even the White House was involved. All of that was good news. Boeing was being defensive, as were the FBI and the Department of Defense. That was to be expected; they were defendant's, after all. We could only pray that whoever controlled the kidnappers would instruct them to release our boys, alive and intact.

Before we left Pegasus for the Captain's House, I used the john at Pegasus, which had one of those old-fashioned pull-chain toilets, where I had another flashback to the mental short-circuit I had experienced at the Metropolitan Bar and Grill—that "flushed down the toilet" connection. But that momentary alignment of random synapse firings produced no useful intelligence, at least nothing I could decipher. Maybe if I got my head out of the toilet, my subconscious would cobble together something useful.

Marilyn Hensel welcomed us with an offer of a cup of coffee while we waited for dinner. We groaned.

"Oh," she said. "Before I forget, the Seattle Police just called. You're to call them right away."

I heard the siren of an approaching patrol car as I dialed the number. A Bainbridge cop who I recognized from my last speeding ticket, Jack Alford, pulled into Marilyn's driveway just as Seattle Police Detective Russo answered the phone.

"The kidnappers called again. At least we think it was them. I'm sorry to say we weren't able to trace the call—our equipment malfunctioned somehow—but the voice sounded like the guy who called that other time. He wanted to know where you were, now that your house was, to use his phrase, 'a pile of stinkin' rubble.' So I told him. I expect you'll be getting a call from them soon, maybe a visit—but a visit seems unlikely. But for sure you'll be getting a call. But don't worry. Some Bainbridge officers will be there shortly. They'll wire up the B&B's phone and they'll stick around in case anyone shows up."

"They're here, Sergeant Russo. They just arrived."

"Good. They're going to wire the Captain's House phone to ring here as well as there. But we won't answer it; we'll just record and trace any calls. If our damned equipment works next time."

"You think they will call us here?"

"Yes. Why else would they have called us? Can you handle a phone call?"

"I guess I don't have any choice."

"Not really. What I meant was, do you think you can keep them on the line long enough to maybe pump them for some information?"

Just that quickly, Russo's words completed my elusive neural connection. As suddenly as a frozen faucet suddenly thawing and spewing frigid water, I knew exactly where Dan had hidden the microfiches. Just as instantly, I also knew exactly what I had to do. I took a deep breath and felt myself calm down. I can't explain it any better than that. Everything was now clear. Where confusion had reigned, certainty now prevailed. Certainty and a growing sense of sureness and calm.

"I'll do my best, Sergeant Russo. But I've one favor to ask."

"Yes?"

"Can you get me a cellular phone? Right away?"

"A cell phone? What for?"

"Because I'm tired of not being available by phone. I need one."

"Oh. Well yeah, that makes sense. I'll get one to you."

Jack Alford, the Bainbridge cop, grabbed my arm. I pulled the phone away from my ear.

"Mine's in the car," Alford said. "You're welcome to it. Number's 206-555-5665.

I nodded my thanks and relayed the phone number to Russo, then rang off.

Soon, Marilyn had dinner ready. Fresh razor clams she'd picked up at the Pike Place Market on her way to the ferry, sautéed in butter with two halved, squeezed lemons and about a dozen cloves of garlic, served over brown rice stir-fried with baby carrots, tiny onions, and zucchini, all picked fresh from her own garden.

Even though my stomach was full of donuts and smoke, I ate like someone coming off a fast.

Maybe all complicated cases like ours break down over time, but maybe not as quickly as ours had. Our case, just a week old and already a jumble of jurisdictional squabbles and internecine rivalries, had fallen into chaos when we filed our civil suit.

Who was in charge? The FBI? Now they were defendants as well as investigators and were busy ducking reporters. The Seattle Police? They were certainly better suited for that role, though they were hampered by their own tactical problems: recalcitrant telephone equipment, detectives shunted aside by the FBI, crime scenes that kept blowing up, civilians like me who hid cards up our sleeves. The Bainbridge Police? Maybe. They had lost an officer, David Welch, so they were fully vested, but they lacked the staff, equipment, and experience to do much more than provide local protection and the odd cellular phone. Port Angeles' boys in khaki—City and County, plus Big Norm of the Park Service—were barely in the picture. Their search of the cabin and local environs had produced a dead trail, and their all-points bulletin for Dan Crawford and his Jeep Cherokee with Japanese mud and snow tires had produced zilch. Dan's Cherokee had gone to ground, apparently. You could take your pick of who was in charge.

So I did: me. I would be in charge. Why not? I had more pieces of the puzzle than anyone, even Em and Alice. They had most of the pieces, but something told me not to share the epiphany I'd just had about Dan's microfiches. I won't even attempt to justify my reasons for holding back that insight—but yes, I do know that it had a lot to do with my own sense of guilt.

For sure, I wasn't going to take them into my confidence about what I would be doing next. I didn't want to have to try to justify myself, for one thing. Then too, I realized it was possible that my epiphany might turn out to be just another wild goose chase. I didn't think so, but I couldn't be absolutely certain until I'd checked it out, myself.

That's all beside the point, because the real reason for my secretiveness was that I *wanted* to do this myself, not so much because I wanted to be able take full credit if everything worked out as it had to, but because I *needed* to be fully responsible if it didn't.

That's a great definition of egocentrism, as well as a pretty fair definition of how men often relate to women, especially women they love.

Enough with the damned introspection, Andy, I told myself. No time for that now. Do what you need to do, and worry about that stuff later.

After dinner, I told Em and Alice that I needed to get away for awhile. "Can I take your Blazer, Alice?"

"Well, sure, but…"

Em shared her alarm. "But what if the kidnappers call?"

I motioned to the Bainbridge cop, sitting by the phone. "Jack? Can you forward calls to this cell phone you gave me?"

He picked up the phone and dialed a couple numbers, waited a few seconds, then added ten more digits. "There," he said. "Now any calls to the Captain's House will automatically go to your cell phone. The phone here won't even ring."

"You can do that?" I said.

"Anyone can. The instructions are in the phone book. It's called 'call forwarding.'"

"Oh," I said. "Well, that's great."

"But now there's no recording device or tracing capability for incoming calls…" he said, looking a little doubtful. "Maybe we shouldn't do that. The fibbies and the Seattle cops will have a fit."

"Let 'em," I said. "Their tracking and recording crap keeps fouling up anyway. And even when it works, all it tells us is that a call was placed from a phone booth in Santa Monica or Timbuktu or someplace. Big effin' help that's been."

Jack Alford held up his hand. "Got an idea. I'll have Qwest record any incoming calls to the phone here at the Captain's House. They should be able to do that easily. And my cell phone—the one you've got—is a Qwest phone too, and I know they keep records of calls placed to cell phones. So we'll have the number of anyone whose call is answered by your cell phone. You go ahead and take your drive, Andy. Don't worry about anything. If anyone calls here, we'll have a record.

And if you need to check in with us, call me on my new cell phone and we can talk privately."

He reached for the phone he'd given me and put his new cell phone number in its memory. "There. You're all set. Just scroll down to 'Jack,' press 'Send,' and my new phone will ring." He demonstrated. His phone rung. "See? Piece a cake."

I looked at Em to see if she was satisfied, and if she was okay with me leaving. Her look told me that she knew I was up to something and that, regardless of what she said, I wouldn't divulge any of it. I saw anger in her eyes, then resignation, then something I prayed I was interpreting correctly: hopeful trust. I hadn't seen that in a long time.

"Just be sure to check in to make sure your phone is working," she said. "We'll talk more when you get back. We'll talk about everything."

I knew what she meant, and she knew that I knew, so we left it at that. I didn't kiss Em good-bye. Had I done so, I know I wouldn't have left alone. She would have been with me.

I said only, "See you later." I hoped I would.

Jack walked out to the Blazer with me. "Got an idea," he said. "Stop by the station when you leave here and have them attach a cell phone antenna to the car. It sticks to the roof or a window with a suction cup. They'll run the lead from the antenna through a window and you can plug it into the cell phone." He showed me the port on the phone. "That'll give you better reception and more range."

I did as he suggested and headed north. I tested the phone halfway to Poulsbo, then again at the Hood Canal Bridge. It worked great. I spoke to Jack both times and he said he would reassure the women that everything was working out just as it should, communications-wise.

Which was true, except for a minor mishap just outside Port Angeles. The new antenna, stuck to the Blazer's back window with a giant suction cup, blew off in the vortex of wind trailing an oncoming 18-wheeler. I managed to stop before the antenna was too badly dinged up. Exhausting two weeks' worth of spit, I managed to moisten the suction cup on the antenna base and get it stuck to the back window again. I called Seattle information to test the phone and got through, but the operator's voice was fading in and out. I was probably at the limit of reception, even with the extra antenna.

At ten o'clock that night, I reached the top of a familiar hill. Less than a week ago, the boys and I had huffed and puffed our way to its crest, pushing a Cwazy Wabbit. Twilight was nearly gone, leaving a quickly darkening crimson curtain, like blood drying, only faster.

I stopped the Blazer at the top of that hill, hoping the elevation and an unobstructed line of sight would compensate for being at the limits of the phone's range. I got through to Jack, barely, but managed to convey that I would be home in a couple hours. He didn't ask where I was.

Through the hiss and static, Jack told me that the women had gone to the Madrona Cafe for dinner and a few drinks. Immediately, I wanted one too.

"No calls from anyone except you," he continued. "But you better let me replace that phone with a better one when you get back. I can barely hear you."

A few minutes later I was at Dan Crawford's cabin. As I expected, the cabin was dark, apparently deserted. The key to the padlock on the door was still in the rain gutter, and the door still opened as easily as it had the day the boys and I had first arrived at Dan's WWIII retreat.

I pushed on the door and it swung in, soundlessly, hitting the wall with a mild thud. A sour smell like tennis shoes left too long in a school locker assailed my nose and made my eyes water. I reached for a light switch before remembering the cabin had no electricity. I should have brought a flashlight. Wait. Wasn't there a Coleman white-gas lantern over the kitchen sink? I headed in that direction and promptly tripped, winding up on my hands and knees. I sat up and kicked out at whatever had tripped me up. I heard a soft, squishy sound and visualized a small animal that had somehow made it into the cabin and been unable to get out again. Probably died of lead poisoning after nibbling on the shutters. That would explain the smell.

I removed my trusty Bic lighter from my pocket and flicked it to life, remembering as I always did when flicking my Bic, a contest some years back. Bic Lighters had provided the first two lines of a limerick, and entrants were to devise the next three lines of complete the limerick, which would appear in a future advertisement. A friend and I came up with this gem:

> *I once knew a pretty good trick,*
> *That began with a flick of my Bic.*
> *Called the "flame-throwing dude,"*
> *I performed in the nude,*
> *'Til I burned off the end of my wick.*

130

We should have won. We would have, if Bic hadn't been so timid.

I held the flaming lighter out as far in front of me as I could while I sat on the floor. The bright yellow flame almost blinded me in the cabin's near-total blackness. Holding the lighter over my head, I got to my feet. A glint of light reflected off something dangling over the sink. The lantern. I headed for it, keeping the lighter raised and sweeping my free hand in front of me as a crude early warning device.

I reached the sink without further mishap, found some matches in a small dish to the left of the sink, and got the lamp going, then returned the Bic to my pants pocket. And immediately groped it out again to keep my thigh from blistering. I tossed the lighter in the sink to cool it off. It made a hissing sound as it landed in a trace of water in the sink strainer.

Aha! A clue! Someone had run water into the sink recently. A closer look revealed some pinkish water standing in the strainer. The lantern cast a lot of light. At first everything seemed to be in order. The table was where it had been, chairs arranged around it neatly. The gun cabinet was in place, as was the rocking chair alongside the fireplace. The floor was covered with numerous feathery dust-balls. The only thing out of place was a short, bent piece of something that looked like a paper-birch limb in the middle of the floor, probably the thing I had tripped over. Not a dead animal, after all. I removed the lantern from its hook over the sink, intent on carrying it to the bedroom to continue my investigation.

As I bent over to pick up the piece of birch kindling, my stomach crawled up my throat.

What I had taken for a limb from a tree was a different sort of limb, the lower half of someone's arm, cleanly severed just below the elbow, probably by an ax. There were no blood stains on the arm. It had been washed clean.

The reason for the pink water in the sink—and for that horrible scream I'd heard on the phone—was evident. But whose arm was it? Rick's? DJ's? Miguel's? No way to tell. The boys all had similar coloring, deep suntans, darkish hair. I could see dark hair on the arm, matted to the skin. By the arrangement of fingers and thumb, I could see it was the lower half of someone's left arm.

I staggered to the door and retched. No clams came up, just an awful, bitter mix of garlic-infused bile. A few moments later I staggered back to the horror on the floor. There was a ring on the third finger of the hand at the end of the arm—a class ring, heavy and golden, with a faceted red stone. Like the ring I had given Rick last year, my old ring from the University of Minnesota, with its pretty but worthless garnet. Rick loved that ring and always wore it.

I would have slid the ring off the finger and checked it more closely, had I been able to. But my hands shook too badly, and I couldn't bring myself to touch the arm. But I bent down until my forehead was almost on the floor and willed myself to focus only on the ring. Just the ring, nothing else. Not the stiffened finger. Not the dead hand. Not the severed arm.

... The severed *left* arm....

I remembered that Rick, a southpaw, wore my ring on his right hand. Tears of shameless gratitude clouded my vision as I read the raised letters surrounding the stone: HARVARD.

Dan Senior's ring. Apparently, right-handed Dan Junior wore his father's ring on his left hand.

I'm not ashamed to tell you that I cried for a good long while. I'd like to be able to tell you that I shed tears over the loss of DJ's left arm. I suppose I did, but mainly I wept in grateful relief that it wasn't Rick's. And I cried because I was absolutely certain that Rick's arm would be next.

I knew I needed to report this right away. To the Seattle Police, through the local authorities. But I couldn't see how it would matter. The combined constabulary hadn't accomplished anything yet. I stumbled over to the table and sat in a chair, my head in my hands, trying to think.

God, I needed a drink. I spotted a can of Coke on a shelf and popped its top, then pulled one long, sour swig until the can was drained. The fizzy acidity scoured the bile from my throat and helped clear my mind. I looked around the cabin again and saw that the gun cabinet had been stripped. All the guns were gone. All the ammo—the little bald-headed soldiers and their box-bivouacked reinforcements—were missing in action. I moved to the bedroom. The mattress had been slashed, as had the two foam pillows. Bedding lay strewn in a heap in the corner of the room. In the loft upstairs, similar shambles: sleeping bags ripped open, their down stuffing scattered as if by a tiny, furious blizzard—the source of the dust balls downstairs.

Obviously, the kidnappers had returned to the cabin to find the microfiches, after cutting off DJ's arm while making that awful recording, leaving his arm as further proof of their determination to get what they wanted.

I finally remembered why I had come: to get what everyone had been looking for. I went out to the Blazer for the tool box Alice always carried in her car. I extracted a pipe wrench from the bottom of the tool box.

A few minutes later, I had twisted the kitchen sink's hand-pump from its pipe, confirming the picture my subconscious mind had supplied. My meeting with Boeing's Smith had provided the trickle of memory—microfilm being flushed down a toilet. But Sergeant Russo of the Seattle Police had opened the tap fully when he asked me to pump the kidnappers for information. At that moment, my mind's eye had produced a three-dimensional image of Dan's cabin, zooming in on a 2,000-gallon water tank—and a hand-pump at the sink.

I felt inside the two-inch-diameter pipe that had connected the pump to the water tank. The microfiches were tucked just inside the end of the pipe. Dan had removed the pump, rolled the thin stack of three-by-five-inch sheets of photographic film into a tight cylinder and slipped them into the pipe. With the pump replaced, the flow of water would be restricted only slightly, with no one the wiser.

I patted the microfiches dry with a kitchen towel and slipped them into my jacket pocket. After putting the pipe wrench away, I returned to the cabin, wrapped the same towel around Dan Junior's arm, then placed the awful bundle in the back of the Blazer, next to the tool box.

When I walked into the Port Angeles PD building, Sergeant Mink was on duty at his desk, dozing. I cleared my throat, startling him awake.

His eyes became saucers as he unrolled the towel I had placed in front of him.

19

I did not show Sergeant Mink the microfiches. I couldn't be sure that turning them over to one police agency wouldn't result in them getting into the hands of the FBI. If that happened, I would have forfeited the only bargaining chip I had, and the kidnappers would have no reason to keep the boys alive. Dan Crawford had died for those white-on-black strips of film, as had an honorable agent named Griffin and a good cop and very good man named Welch. And now DJ had given up an arm. Those microfiche bargaining chips were well-steeped in blood.

Considering the sudden trauma I had injected into Sergeant Mink's dreams, he allowed me to leave with rather more grace than I had shown him.

"I'll call Jane Crawford," he said as I left. "Unless you want to..." he said, hope in his eyes.

I thanked him for making the call. I shouldn't have chickened out. It would have been easier for Jane to hear the news from me, but I salved my conscience with the knowledge that the news would be devastating, regardless. At the time it didn't feel like such a self-serving rationalization.

I stepped back inside the police station. "But don't call my wife. I'll call her myself. I've got a phone in the car."

"Okay, I'll call the Bainbridge cop...I mean, officer... whatshisname?"

"Alford. Jack Alford. But tell him not to tell my wife."

As soon as I was within hailing range, I picked up the phone to call Em—and at that same moment the phone rang. Apparently Em had the same idea. The phone's reception was bad, but her anger came through five by five, as we used to say on our military squawk boxes.

"Where are you Andy? You should be home by now."

Looked like Mink had told Alford to keep my little discovery secret. I was tempted to just blurt out the story right there on the phone, but remembered that it would be recorded by Qwest, so all I said was, "I'll tell you all about it. Meet me at Poulsbo, at the Sands. I'll get there as fast as I can."

Fifteen minutes later the phone rang again. This time it was Jack Alford. Reception was better and he spoke quickly.

"The kidnappers called, just after your wife and Mrs. Sharp left for the Sands. I don't know why the call didn't go directly to you—to your cell phone. I guess you can't 'call forward' calls from a landline to a cell phone. Sorry about that."

Before I could say anything, Jack continued. "Anyway, I didn't know just what to do, Andy. The kidnappers said they would speak only to you, so I gave them your cell number.

You're kinda on your own here, buddy, but try to find out whatever you can, because I also found out there's some glitch with Qwest taping calls to cell phones."

I heard Jack take a deep breath before he continued. "I'm sorry, man. Really sorry, but you need to try to find out where they are calling from. I heard some birds in the background when they called here. Sounded like the hoot owls around our farmhouse in Michigan when I was a kid."

I'd been holding my breath and let it out, trying to invoke some calm. "I'll do what I can, Jack. As soon as I talk to them I'll call you back. In the meantime, please call the girls at the Sands and fill them in, and tell them I'll see them soon."

I put the phone back in its cradle and pulled the car to the side of the road, where I sat, quivering. If I was closer to Poulsbo, I would try to make it to the Sands, so Em could take the call from the kidnappers. Or Alice. Jesus. Anyone but me.

"Arrgh!" I screamed. Then cursed my cowardice and slapped myself across the check. Hard. Twice. And tried to regain the calm I'd felt before leaving the Captain's House.

The cell phone rang.

If you haven't already tumbled to it, there is something you need to know. I'm no hero. I've always felt that confrontation and danger are caused by decisions deliberately made—and best avoided. That's why I left the Air Force. The tough got going and I got going when their backs were turned.

For the most part, I've been happy living that way. Until Em got fed up with my avoidance behavior and left in disgust. Soon, I'd have to do something about that.

I still prefer to avoid difficulty. But let me tell you, your "druthers" become way less important when bad things happen and your options dwindle. When you're backed into a corner, your convictions are no longer so convincing. Your usual precautions fade, your usual restraints fall away. You spend less time thinking about consequences; you just act—because you have no alternative. Sometimes I think that's how all heroism occurs.

Maybe that's why all those Aussie troops at Gallipoli crawled out of their trenches and into a fusillade of bullets, even if it did take some prodding with bayonets held by their blindly obedient officers, all of whom remained behind in the trenches. Those soldiers had no choice. Their commanding officers did: they could have disobeyed the orders of *their* superiors and protected those soldiers in their care. Had they done so, their men would not have been sent into a futile battle—and that would have constituted true heroism. But they didn't. They obeyed their orders, sent their men to a certain death because they feared their superiors. And so their men—heroes, one and all—died.

Maybe that's the only kind of courage there really is: doing what you have to do, whether you've chosen it or not, then trying to make the best of it.

Feeling like a doomed Aussie grunt, my cheek still smarting from the prodding of my own bayonet, I felt anything but heroic. But I did feel...different. I was beginning to regain the calmness, hope, and glimmerings of confidence I had felt at the Captain's House when I realized where Dan Crawford had hid the film.

Okay. I could do this. I could play this out.

I answered the phone.

"Hello." My voice was steady.

"Where are the microfiches, Eastman?"

"I have them."

"You do?"

Score one for me. "Yes. I'm ready to make a trade—the microfiches for the boys. Are you?" I took their moment of silence as a good sign. Maybe these guys were less competent than they'd seemed.

"We'll call you back in five minutes."

"No dice. No deal, unless I talk to my son. Right now. Put him on or you can read the microfiches in tomorrow's newspapers."

The next voice was the sweetest and saddest sound I had ever heard.

"Dad?" Rick's voice was high-pitched and a little shaky.

"Are you all right, son?"

"I'm okay. But DJ…"

"I know. Is he alive? And Miguel?"

"Yeah, they're both okay. They've got Deej all doped up on something."

"Okay. Now listen carefully, Rick. I'm going to ask you some 'yes' or 'no' questions, and I want you to sniff like you're coming down with a cold."

"I *am* coming down with a cold."

"All the better. Give me one sniff for 'yes,' two for 'no.' Understand?"

Sniff.

"Good. Now, are you in Seattle?"

Sniff, sniff.

"Washington state?"

Sniff.

"Olympic Peninsula?"

Sniff.

"Near the Crawfords' cabin?"

Sniff.

"Would you be able to see someone if they were driving to the cabin?"

Sniff, sniff.

"How many kidnappers are there, Rick? Sniff once for each one…."

Sniff, sniff, then, *Sniff, sniff.*

So, there were four of them.

And one of them grabbed the phone from Rick. "All right," he said. "Here's what we will do…"

"Go to hell. We'll do this my way or not at all. Is that clear?" Another pause, without a response, so I told him what they had to do: where we would meet to make the exchange, and when.

"Agreed?" I said.

A brief pause, then, "Yes. Fine."

"Repeat it back to me, so I know there won't be any fuck-up."

"Don't worry. There won't be."

"Repeat it back, asshole."

So he repeated it all back, in a voice that I hoped was loud enough for Rick to hear. "Now, put my son back on the phone."

"Negatory. You've had your little chat. Or your little cry, by the sound of it."

"Okay, the deal's off."

"Don't push your luck, Eastman. Any funny business and the boys are dead."

Then Rick was back on the line. I spoke more quickly than before, eager to get everything said. "Listen carefully," I said. You heard him say what's going to happen?"

Sniff.

"Good. Here's what you need to do." It took only a few seconds to tell Rick what the boys had to do to make my plan work. "Got all that?"

Sniff.

"Okay, Rick. That's good. Not much longer, and you guys will be free. And you'll be all right. I…I love you, Rick."

"I love you too, dad. But dad?"

"Yeah?"

"If anything goes wrong, I'll still love you." He spoke that last message in the clear, un-coded, a barely audible whisper, from his heart straight to mine.

"I know Rick. I know that. But nothing will go wrong, I promise."

If it was the last thing I ever did, I would keep my promise.

20

I made three calls on the cell phone as I drove toward Poulsbo, the first to Jack Alford.

"They haven't called yet, Jack," I lied. "I'll be at the Sands with the girls if they call you back. I'll bring the cell phone in with me."

Then I called a Seattle number and got a promise of continued cooperation, then got the same promise when I dialed the number of a five-acre ranchette in Sequim.

Wild Bill had expected my call. "We gonna go get 'em, Andy?"

"You bet." I told him how and where—and when. He vowed to do his part. We finished the conversation just as I steered the Blazer into the parking lot of the Sands.

"Not a word to anyone, Bill. Understood?"

"Betcha."

For the next little while, I was of two minds. Jack Alford had already called Em and Alice and told them that the kidnappers hadn't reached me. So I didn't have to repeat that particular lie. Instead, I could tell them the truth—some of it, anyway.

I suppose I should have felt like a cold, calculating asshole, but I didn't, even as I told them about finding the microfiches, but neglected to mention the call from the kidnappers. Even as I told them about finding Dan's arm in the cabin, but didn't mention talking to Rick.

I didn't dare tell them anything about what I planned to do, and I watched for signs of strained credulity. I saw plenty. But I could not worry about that now.

While part of my mind was parsing one reality with Em and Alice: the right here and the right now, I was also previewing tomorrow's live-action feature, which had already begun with tonight's first-reel phone call from the kidnappers and my talk with Rick, followed by my second-reel phone call to Wild Bill.

The stage was set, but third reel—the denouement—was still being scripted and wouldn't unspool until tomorrow.

Em and Alice had blanched when I told them about finding Dan Senior's Harvard ring on the hand attached to DJ's right arm. Like me, both were relieved it wasn't Rick's or Miguel's arm, which made me feel a little less hypocritical. I'm sure both of them wondered why I had been so relatively unemotional in telling the tale. Perhaps they attributed it to my overloaded emotions. Had they known the real reason—that a severed arm paled in comparison to the import of my conversation with Rick and the plans I'd made with Wild Bill for events that would unfold at noon tomorrow—er, later today—my calmness would have been understandable. Compared with what was to come, what else mattered?

A more perfect man would have confided in them. I'm not that man. My reasons for keeping them in the dark wouldn't have withstood much scrutiny, so I didn't do any scrutinizing. I knew that if I even hinted at my plan, they would talk me out of it. I could not let that happen.

After a nightcap in the bar we headed back to the island. Alice drove the borrowed Pontiac so Em and I could ride together in the Blazer.

Em rested her hand on my thigh. "I understand why you had to get out for awhile. You had to go back to the cabin, didn't you? Not just to follow your hunch about the microfiches, but just to be back where the boys were taken, to see if being there would help you figure out how to get them back. Am I right?"

"Yeah," I said. "You always have known me better than I know myself."

"Yes. I do. But I think I've still got a lot to learn."

Indeed. I hoped and prayed that what Em would learn about me tomorrow wouldn't completely destroy the gains we seemed to be making as a couple these last few days.

We spent the rest of the trip in an amiable silence, the two of us feeling close, but also needing to be alone with our thoughts. We went straight to bed at the Captain's House.

Marilyn had laid out pajamas on our bed. Flannel they were—bulky, baggy things, pink and blue. All they lacked were bunny feet and puffy tails. Under normal circumstances, they would have been hilarious. As it was, we didn't keep them on long, cuddling like a pair of spoons. I didn't feel like talking, and although I knew that Em knew something big was on my mind, I also knew she wouldn't pry. She knew I wasn't yet ready to talk about it right now—but that I would. And that would be okay. Whatever weaknesses there were in our marriage—and there were many—I knew that a lack of trust in me by Em wasn't one of them. She knew I was in a state of barely controlled panic that would end only when Rick was back with us, safe and sound. She believed that whatever I would do, it would be the right thing, even if I did it wrong. I knew that in my heart at that moment, and I also knew that I loved my wife more than life itself. Way more.

We would get through this, I vowed. Whatever happened, all of us would get through this.

After awhile we reversed positions and Em kneaded some of the knots out of my neck and shoulders. And after another while, we made love, quietly, deliberately, with slowly building intensity. Without words, we rocked in the cradle of the gods, joined as one, not saying everything we needed to say, but everything we *could* say—and perfectly communicating everything we felt.

Locked in that oldest and most vital embrace, our bodies and souls spoke for us, affirming our identity, confirming our love, more than doubling our strength for whatever lay ahead.

Em drifted off to sleep, her breathing peaceful and even. I cuddled her backside and grabbed for sleep that hovered just out of reach. After an hour or so, I eased out of that saggy old double bed, slipped back into my plush blue jammies, and padded down the stairs. Jack Alford was asleep on the couch in the living room, a knitted afghan tucked under his chin like a large bib. His light snores didn't falter as I slipped out the front door.

From the front porch, Bainbridge Island's moon-lit harbor looked like a photographer's silver iodide glossy black and white print. Gazing past the shadowed angularity of the buildings housing Pegasus Coffee Shop and the Island Chandlery, I could see the shrouded sails of a tidy fleet of sailboats, mingled with the antenna masts of motor cruisers. No breeze or wave disturbed the stillness of the harbor. Maybe not a black and white print—perhaps a larger-than-life Impressionist painting. I smoked several cigarettes and finally returned to bed.

21

Marilyn outdid herself at breakfast: home fries, thick-sliced bacon, lightly scrambled eggs, sourdough toast, her own home-made blackberry jam. This was our first visit to her bed and breakfast, and I think she wanted to make an extra special impression, partly because it was our first time as formal guests and partly…well, mostly because of the situation.

She had called us down to breakfast at six o'clock. I had been asleep for about two hours, and looked it. Em, on the other hand, was radiant. But then, Em always looks radiant. We sat at the large butcher-block eating counter in Marilyn's kitchen. After pouring our coffee and before taking my first bite of toast, I made my announcement.

"Did I mention that I promised Wild Bill Crawford that I would meet him for lunch in Sequim after I see Dale Kennedy this morning?" A quick mouthful of toast slathered with jam gave me an excuse not to elaborate.

"Will you be seeing Mommie Dearest, too?" Em asked. I nodded. "Tell her how sorry we are…about DJ.…"

"Of course."

"What about DJ?" Marilyn asked. Em and Alice filled her in.

"Oh my God, oh that poor child. How awful!" Marilyn worked with kids in Seattle but had none of her own, a situation about to be remedied. Soon she would be adopting two kids, an abused brother and sister, both in their early teens, not much younger than Rick, Miguel and Dan Junior. "We've got to do something to help Jane. We've got to."

Her brow creased for only a few seconds. "I know. Let's *all* go up to Sequim. We'll take Jane and the kids and go out to the beach or someplace. I mean, life goes on, right?"

Jack Alford came up with a cell phone for Marilyn's car and had already given me a new one for the Blazer, so it looked like I could take off early. I breathed an almost invisible sigh of relief that didn't quite escape Em's notice. She raised her eyebrows, an invitation for me to elaborate.

"I'll be glad when this is over," I said. "Waiting is hard."

Everyone agreed. Even Jack Alford, who had been on the case only for a day.

At 6:45, I was on the road. Em, Alice, and Marilyn would leave an hour or so later, in Marilyn's Eurovan. Em called me on her cell phone as they left.

"These things are fun," she said. "It sounds like you're right next door."

I wasn't. I was past the turnoff to Port Townsend, nearing Sequim. But I agreed. I could see how we would be spending at least part of the advance from my books. Maybe we'd buy a new car too, maybe one of those slick Audi all-wheel-drive wagons that adjust their suspension height to road conditions; I've coveted one of those for a couple years now. Maybe I could get them to install a hands-free cell-phone as part of the deal....

Pleasant thought. But only a momentary one. I had to hurry. I had already stopped at Dale Kennedy's to see if he had a microfiche reader. He did, wonder of wonders, and would print out hard copies of the contents of the microfiches. I waited a precious few extra minutes while he made a duplicate set of the negatives for himself.

"Don't worry about a thing, Andy," he told me as I left. "I'll get the hard copies and negatives delivered right away. By nine at the latest."

At Sequim, I found Wild Bill waiting in his pickup at the end of his long, curving driveway, just out of sight of the house. He pointed at me, then at his chest, then out his windshield and away he went, all four wheels on his F-150 spewing gravel. I followed, and in a few minutes we arrived at a self-storage complex, one of many that look like a set of garages for the former Bhagwan Shree Rajneesh's former fleet of Rolls Royces in the former Rajneesh, Oregon—now back to its old and more durable name: Antelope.

143

Wild Bill stopped in front of one of the garage doors and had it unlocked and raised before I got the Blazer stopped. We stepped inside and Bill pulled the door down, then pulled the cord for the overhead light.

The space was crammed. Wild Bill eased himself between stacks of treasures to an upright trunk about five feet tall, three feet wide, and a foot deep. He pulled a key out of his overalls and unlocked the trunk.

Inside was an arsenal that would make Rick drool, including some exotic pieces I recognized from Rick's *Soldier of Fortune* magazines. Machine pistols, mainly.

Together we lugged the case to the Blazer and heaved it in the back. Wild Bill left his pickup at the storage place and rode with me to the Crawford cabin. It was a fast, silent ride. Wild Bill felt no need to talk; neither did I. Gary Cooper would have felt right at home.

We left the Blazer parked at the turnoff to the cabin and we carried the crate of guns between us down the gravel road. Sunlight was bathing the cabin as we arrived, the last of the early morning dew steaming off its roof. Freshly applied Day-Glo orange crime scene tape stretched across the cabin door.

"How much time we got?" Bill said, as we set the box down at the door.

"Less than three hours." I said.

"Oughta do it," he said.

"Oughta," I said.

It was nine-thirty. By high noon it would be hot.

22

Wild Bill ripped the bright yellow CRIME SCENE tape off the door and stuffed it in his pocket. "Sure as Hades got that right," he said.

I said, "Key's over the door…"

"…In the gutter," he finished, fishing it out and opening the lock. "Ever'body always puts 'em there. 'Less there's a welcome mat."

We pushed the door open, then retrieved the trunk of weapons. Lugging it down the road and into the house had left me short of breath and I stepped outside for a breather. And a cigarette. Bill joined me.

"Purty place," he said, looking around. "Purty day, too." Indeed it was, one of those sunny, calm mornings that punctuate the frequent rains of June with occasional exclamation points of extraordinary beauty and clarity.

I guessed my senses were heightened by a shortage of sleep—or more likely, by knowledge of the upcoming confrontation. I don't know. For whatever reason, I noticed things. Birds sang louder than usual. A whisper of wind swayed the treetops in a graceful minuet I rarely noticed. Rays of sunlight highlighted a tapestry of alternately brilliant, then shadowy tones of green and yellow and blue in the tree canopy and the sparse underbrush.

Wild Bill was looking too. Then he stomped his cigarette into the dirt and turned quickly toward the cabin. "Come on," he said. "No time t' waste."

Wild Bill spent the next half hour in an economical explanation of exactly enough and no more than I needed to know about each of the weapons available. He recommended an H&K machine pistol for me because of its predictable firing pattern and mild recoil.

"Better 'n those damn Uzis that spray all over the place."

For backup I would have a shotgun, a pump-action twelve-gauge whose barrel had been sawed off at the end of the fore-stock. The shotgun would come in handy for close-quarter shooting.

"But ya shun't hafta use it. They won't be gettin' that close. If they do, aim it right here." He poked a finger at center of his chest. "That's where ya point yer pistol, too."

He showed me how to reload the shotgun and change out the clips in the H&K. He had me practice with both pieces until I could reload them with my eyes closed, almost fast enough to satisfy him. I would have three spare magazines for the H&K and a full box of buck-shot shells for the shotgun, besides the shell already chambered and the three waiting in its tubular magazine.

"Reckon that'll do her," he said. For himself he selected an ancient Marlin 30-30, a lever action with a two-and-a-half power scope. An identical twin to my old deer hunting rifle.

"Killed a whole lotta deer with that one," he said. "Got her sighted in at a hundred yards, so I'll hafta remember t' aim a couple inches low. They'll be closer 'n that."

He nodded to himself to commit that to memory. I figured he wouldn't forget. His back-up weapons were a pair of pearl-handled re-volvers, .44 caliber Colts, I think. With the six-guns strapped to his belt and the rifle tipped over his shoulder, he looked a lot like an older ver-sion of Matt Dillon. I looked like Festus. I felt like Miss Kitty.

"Well, son, this is it. We're as ready as we'll ever be."

He looked at me and cocked an eye, probably a little dubious at what he saw. I set the H&K on the table, the print of my sweaty palm clearly visible on its stubby fore-grip.

Wild Bill reached into an inside pocket of his overalls and pulled out a beat-up flask and handed it to me. I felt even more like Festus but a little less like Miss Kitty after a long pull on it. Scotch. Matt Dil-lon would have favored red-eye, whatever that was. Festus would have taken anything he could get, like me at that point. I was grateful for the scotch.

"Walker Black," he said. "Small flask. Don't hold much, so I get the best." I handed the flask to him and he held it out toward the door of the cabin. "Happy huntin'," he said, then took a short swig. He capped the flask and returned it to his pocket, then patted it into place, familiarly.

"Happy hunting," I mimicked shakily.

"Yep. That's what it'll be, all right." He looked at me again and narrowed his eyes. "It'll help t' think of 'em as animals, Andy. 'Cause that's what they are, rabid animals what gotta be put down."

I nodded, though I thought he was being a little unfair to animals. I'd think of them as rabid predators—foam-spewing hyenas. A pack of four.

We moved over to the fireplace and sat with our backs against the cool rock, staring out the open door. We waited. It was ten-thirty.

23

Our brains are adept, powerful, and complex, as fast as the swiftest computers, capable of near-instantaneous computation and subtle simultaneous comparisons of dissimilar "what-if" scenarios. They need very little to keep operating: a little fuel, some oxygen, occasional water, a few trace minerals—that's about it. They don't complain when overworked or overloaded, either; they just pause and recharge. Shortly before eleven o'clock, I fell asleep.

Wild Bill awakened me five minutes later, to a bad case of the shakes. My dream wasn't a new one. I was back in my bunker in Hue, ducking a cacophonous fury of incoming mortar and rockets—interlocking mega-dB concussive waves felt as much as heard, sensations even the best Dolby surround-sound systems only feebly approximate. I hadn't visited that horrific hidey-hole in a long time, but it was as vivid right then, twenty-plus years later, as the original. For a brief moment, stuck between states of consciousness, I was *there* in that hot, wet hell of Indochina.

Then I saw Wild Bill's face and remembered—and decided that Hue might have been preferable to *this* firing line. Back then, I had only myself to worry about. Now, Rick's life was at stake, and Miguel's and DJ's, as well as my own. And now I'd added Wild Bill to the lineup. I walked outside to shake off the fear. The sun was nearing its apex and the wind had died down. The day was not nearly as beautiful as it had been just a short while ago. The air was a whole lot hotter. It was way too warm for my jacket but I decided to keep it on, because it was black and my open-necked sport shirt was a pale blue, my tee shirt white. Better to not wave a white flag at the hyenas when they arrived.

Bill moved to his chosen post, a large Douglas-fir standing at the end of the driveway. Because the tree had spent its entire life in the open, its lower branches were full, nearly reaching the ground. About 30 inches in diameter and 100 feet in height, it deserved a final two weeks of glory as the nation's Christmas tree in D.C.

Wild Bill slung his rifle over his shoulder and started climbing the tree, with more assurance than I could have mustered. Thirty feet up, he perched on the branch he selected. From there, he would have a clear view and an open field of fire from the head of the driveway to the front door of the cabin, with just enough smaller branches to shelter him from view. He would be unnoticed from the ground, unless he did something stupid, like falling off the limb.

I would be stationed inside the cabin when they arrived, my field of vision and field of fire circumscribed by the cabin doorway. Big enough, I hoped.

Wild Bill settled onto his perch, comfortable and relaxed. He got out the flask again, took a short snort, and tossed it down to me.

"You need this liquid courage 'bout as much as me, Andy." I immediately killed most of what was left. I brushed my lips on my shirt-sleeve and gave him a thumbs-up sign, then went inside the cabin.

I occupied myself by rigging my signal for the boys. I tied a length of twine to the interior shutter on the window and gave it a test tug. The shutter swung inward. When the boys saw that, they were to fall to the ground immediately and roll away from their captors. Bill and I would open fire as soon as the boys were in the clear.

We would make no announcements. We would shout no warning. We were not there to negotiate. We were not seeking the runner-up Mister Congeniality award.

I pushed the shutter closed and reclaimed my post inside the door, kneeling just inside the deep shadows. I figured the kidnappers would see the flash from the barrel of my weapon before they saw me. I visualized how it would unfold. They would drive up. They would pause a moment before getting out of their vehicle, probably some kind of four-wheel-drive.

When they were clear of the vehicle, I would yank on the twine, the shutter would swing open, and the boys would fall to the ground and roll out of harm's way. Then Wild Bill and I would blow the four kidnappers into bloody bits. It should work just that way. It had to.

I went to the sink and threw up the scotch. It was eleven-forty.

24

For the next twenty minutes I knelt on one knee, then the other, then stood and stretched for a few seconds to relieve the twanging tautness of my thigh and calf muscles. Then knelt again, trying not to focus on all the very logical reasons to be someplace else.

For one thing, I wasn't equipped to be a vigilante, emotionally or physically. I had been a fair shot in the Air Force, but that was a very long time ago, and you already know my feelings about guns and my bent towards pacifism. So what was I doing with a stubby machine pistol in my hands that made my old M-16 look like a pea-shooter? With spare clips tucked into my belt, for Christ's sake, and a sawed-off shotgun at my feet. A pudgy Barney Fife playing Rambo. Ludicrous. The muscles in my entire body would fit into Sylvester Stallone's right biceps—and he's left-handed.

My legs quivered. My palms were so sweaty I wondered if I shouldn't just drop the gun right now and save myself the embarrassment later. My mouth tasted of puke. I took a small sip of scotch and swished it around, swallowed, slowly exhaled. My physical shortcomings seemed less noticeable.

What we were doing was illegal as hell. Just handling one of these fully automatic weapons was grounds for serious prison time. Even if we somehow managed to kill all the kidnappers, which at the moment seemed iffy, even with the element of surprise, the cops would probably charge us with premeditated murder. You don't deliberately conspire to set up an ambush, even when the ambushees are killers. Do you?

Well....

Yes. You do. You do whatever you have to do when your kid's life is at stake. That's the pure and simple truth of it. Normal rules of civilized behavior don't apply. Moral dictums and philosophical convictions be damned: someone threatens your kid with death, you kill him and you gut him, and you string him up, and that's that. That's what Wild Bill and I planned to do. We weren't seeking the legal system's "justice" any more. We didn't want to see these assholes get a fair trial. We wanted them dead. What would happen later would happen later.

I took another sip of the scotch, then set the flask aside. I kneeled, raised the H&K to a firing position, took another deep breath and let it our halfway, like Wild Bill had suggested. About half of my tremors disappeared. "Think of them as animals," Wild Bill had said.

"Rabid hyenas," I muttered. I lowered the weapon and looked at my watch. Both hands straight up. Noon.

I flinched as I heard a vehicle crunch its way up the road toward the cabin. A second later, a flash of sunlight glinted off a chrome bumper and the vehicle became visible, a Jeep Wagoneer, the old four-door, nine-passenger model, dirty brown in color, with windows so dark you could hardly see through them. The Wagoneer rolled up the road slowly, cautiously, stopping about twenty feet short of the lowest branches of Wild Bill's tree.

I couldn't see much through the Wagoneer's windows but I thought I could make out four adult-sized shapes.

The engine died. The ticking of the cooling engine was clearly audible. The doors remained closed. Inside were our boys, presumably down on the floor, out of sight. Four cautious hyenas were taking their time, checking things out, sniffing for traps, not ready to emerge until they were satisfied they were in no danger.

"Come on..." I muttered. "Come on...."

Hidden beyond the dark line of shadow inside the open cabin door, I grew cold to my core, as if I were standing in a dark and prehistorically chilly cave, my club raised high, my prey about to creep within reach.

The right front door of the Wagoneer eased open a few inches, and the barrel of a club resembling my own poked out. Then a booted foot, and a leg clad in green camouflage khaki. Finally, the other leg. The door swung open suddenly and a large man rolled quickly into a patch of blackberries lining the drive. He stayed prone and hidden, oblivious of thorns. I couldn't see him at all from my vantage point. Could Bill?

A second later, the opposite door opened and the driver, similarly camouflaged, executed a similar flop and roll into his own patch of briars.

Almost immediately, both back doors popped open. The first person out on my side was Rick, followed closely and held even more closely by a slender man about my age and height, who held the business end of his machine pistol tightly against Rick's temple. A short, fat man got out the other rear door, with Miguel in front of him, an identical pistol pressed against Miguel's head. Both men were attired in green camouflage identical to their compatriots in the vines. Billed caps shaded their eyes from the sun, but they wore no sunglasses.

The man holding Rick frog-walked him toward the cabin door, keeping Rick in front as a shield. About thirty feet from the open door the man stopped and stared directly at me. I froze, praying that I remained invisible to him, that the sunlight outside had shrunk his pupils to pinpoints so he couldn't see me crouched in the cabin's shadows.

Miguel's gunman followed Rick's until both boys were standing side by side, guns at the back of their heads. In a moment, the other two kidnappers emerged from their thorny hiding places and stood flanking their unholy brothers, but facing away from me. Their upper bodies rotated slowly, side to side, along with their guns, covering the area away from the cabin, the direction from which they expected an ambush.

"The Crawford kid is in the back of the wagon." The guy holding Rick made the announcement, this time without the "Godfather" accent. "He's weak, but he's alive."

This wasn't going according to plan. I hadn't visualized guns pressed against the boys' heads. And was DJ really in the back of the car? With another gun against his head? No, that would make five bad guys, and Rick had sniffed only four times. I *think* it was four times. It was, wasn't it?

I had to do something to move the boys out of the line of fire. But what?

What I did wasn't in the script Bill and I had rehearsed. I yelled as loud as I could.

"Drop your guns right now!"

They looked like soldiers caught in a Viet Cong ambush, expecting fire to rain in from all sides. The one holding Rick pushed him away, to open up his line of fire, I suppose, and the guy holding Miguel pushed him to the side, towards Wild Bill's tree. All four men crouched, a maneuver I remember from 'Nam, then rotated slowly from side to side, covering all possible angles of attack, their guns sweeping the jungle for signs of movement.

I yanked on the shutter twine with all my might. The cord snapped. But I had jarred the shutter's equilibrium just enough that it began to swing in, ever so slowly. Rick and Miguel, already on their hands and knees, flopped face down into the dirt and started rolling further away from their captors.

Wild Bill fell out of the tree.

25

Wild Bill Crawford dropped to his death without uttering so much as an "Aw, shucks." I don't know why he fell out of the tree. Maybe he had a heart attack or a stroke, or maybe he fell accidentally while raising his gun to fire. Maybe he fell deliberately. I suppose it's immaterial. Why he fell is less important than the fact that he did fall, landing twenty feet behind the kidnappers, directly in front of their Jeep.

He didn't cry out, but his lanky body made a terrific racket as it crashed down through the branches. The kidnappers' reaction was swift. They sprayed Wild Bill with dozens of bullets before he hit the ground.

I jumped into the opening of the doorway and fired a full clip of shells at the kidnappers' backs, right to left. Like dominos, but less orderly, they tumbled into a bloody heap. I dropped the H&K, grabbed the shotgun, and ran toward the wounded hyenas.

Rick got to his feet, looked at me, then at the carnage. Miguel didn't stand up; he just sat on his butt and rocked back and forth, his face buried in his hands.

Rick said, "Are they dead?" He meant the killers. There was no doubt of Bill's condition.

"Yeah, I think so." I prodded each of them with the toe of my shoe, a formality learned from too many cops and robbers shows. There was no need to roll them over. They were very still, and with so many visible entry wounds in their backs, I didn't need to see the bloody gore of exploded chests.

But Rick and Miguel were alive, and we knelt together in a tripartite hug, none of us able to say much.

"Better see how DJ is," I finally remembered. We opened the tailgate on the Wagoneer. Dan Junior was curled in a fetal position. His eyes flicked open then closed again, with no sign of recognition. He looked so heavily drugged that I doubted the shooting had done much more than punctuate his nightmares with some extreme sound effects.

The stump that used to be Dan's left arm was swaddled in a professional looking bandage that showed no blood. His forehead felt clammy and cool, and I tried to remember what that meant. Shock, I guessed. I told Miguel to stay with DJ, in case he awakened. Rick and I walked over to Wild Bill's body.

Bill had landed on his back. Miraculously, the bullets had spared his head, and his face bore an expression incongruously peaceful in repose. His eyes, thank God, were closed. His body....Oh God. His body was a mess. I couldn't begin to count the number of entry and exit wounds. I wasn't about to. Rick laid his jacket across Bill's chest. I did the same with mine.

"Did he do it on purpose, dad? Falling out of the tree like that?"

"I don't know. I just don't know."

I never will know, but I choose to believe that Rick was right, that Bill had fallen deliberately, just to distract the killers long enough so I could shoot them. The final act of a true hero.

"Uh...Dad?"

I looked at Rick and waited for his question. He didn't say anything. He just looked down at my right hand. I followed his gaze and saw that I was still clutching the shotgun by its pistol grip.

I knelt and placed the shotgun across Bill's chest.

Then I stood up and started to shake, helplessly, a human aspen leaf in fall's first furious storm. My entire body shuddered. Rick put his arms around me and held me as tightly as he could. I could feel him shaking too, but less than me.

"Thanks, dad." His voice broke. I didn't reply, just held him close.

We were still clutching each other when the reporter's cars arrived, followed a few minutes later by patrol cars and an ambulance, their combined sirens an intense, atonal requiem.

26

The press was remarkably balanced in its coverage of the carnage, despite five bodies laying on the ground, riddled with 85 bullets, 69 in Bill Crawford alone, according to the coroner's eventual count of deformed slugs rattling around in a stainless steel trays. Considering the fact that the whole damn massacre had been created by entirely illegal weapons, with most of the killing done by an entirely unlicensed gunman who had just sued everyone in sight, *any* media restraint would have been phenomenal.

Had Chief Able of the Port Angeles PD had his way, press coverage would have been prohibited entirely. But since he had been alerted by the press himself, and had arrived a few moments after they did, his ability to control of the crime scene was marginalized.

Tom MacDonald of the *Seattle Times* reminded him of that, after the chief had sent Dan Crawford Junior off to the hospital and had finished questioning me and the boys.

"Okay, chief. My turn. Remember, you wouldn't even be here if I hadn't called you."

Able didn't like being reminded. "Make it brief, then. And stay away from the bodies."

"No problem."

MacDonald led Miguel, Rick, and me into the cabin and sat us down at chairs around the table. "Tell me what happened." He jotted rapid notes as he listened. The boys described their abduction, which had occurred scant minutes after I'd left them alone in the cabin. They had been kept in another cabin on tribal land in the Hoh Rain Forest, a long way from the scene of the crime. That was where Dan Junior's arm had been chopped off with an ax—and where a dog had been neutered.

I supplied MacDonald with the few details he didn't already have. We'd kept him informed right along, but now I told him about finding the microfiche and told him printouts of their contents were probably waiting for him in his office.

"Did you look at them?" he asked.

"No, but I know they contain a list of blackmail targets exploited by Boeing to get more government contracts. That's what you'll find."

MacDonald had alerted the local CBS affiliate in Seattle before he left for the cabin. His deal with them prescribed that he would do all the on-camera interviewing. I wondered if he was considering a permanent shot at the CBS Evening News. Good-bye Nathan, hello MacDonald.

After quickly reviewing his notes, MacDonald conducted his interview of us right away, leading us skillfully through our stories once again. The video camera operator had moved us outside and posed us several feet away from the bodies, so the bloodied corpses would be just a suggestive blur in the background. The interview lasted about ten minutes, concluding when Chief Able started waving his arms in the background. Tom MacDonald hadn't yet got to his questions about the microfiche-Boeing-extortion connection. He was disappointed.

"More on this story later today," MacDonald concluded, the cameraman zooming in on his face.

As it would turn out, Chief Able pulling the plug on the interview would be a fortunate intervention.

While Rick, Miguel, and I were giving our umpteenth explanation to Chief Able, the final iteration at his police station, the rest of his Port Angeles police department was trying to locate Em, Alice, Jane, and Gladys Crawford, without success. They weren't at the Crawford ranchette in Sequim, and the cops hadn't been able to reach them on the cellular phone in Marilyn Hensel's car, either. As it happened, the battery in their cellular phone had pooped out.

When Chief Able finally dismissed us, the boys and I joined the search. Driving toward Sequim, I remembered their plans for a picnic, and figured I knew where they would be.

I was right. We found them chasing crabs at Dungeness Spit, wading in the shallows at low tide, way out beyond the logs littering the upper fringe of the beach. I honked the horn on the Blazer to get their attention. They peered toward us, shading their eyes against the setting sun, then came on the run, Gladys lagging behind. It looked like a try-out for of those slo-mo TV commercials with lovers running at each other, where you half expect to see them collide and bounce apart, bloody-nosed, thoroughly concussed.

I gave Em a big hug, then let her at Rick. I walked toward Gladys Crawford, and I'm sure my face betrayed my horrible news. Mommie Dearest stood between us, looking from me to her mother-in-law, then back at me. I reached for her hand as I got to her. "Danny's okay," I said. She slumped against me and I pulled her along with me toward Gladys.

When we reached Gladys, she grabbed both of us with hands that were small, fragile and very, very warm.

"Bill's dead, isn't he?"

"Oh, my God," Jane said, looking at me with a look that begged a denial.

"He saved our lives," I said. "None of us would be alive, but for Bill...."

I faltered. I couldn't actually say he was dead. I didn't have to. He hadn't come back with us and so Gladys knew. Oh yes, she knew. She nodded once and gripped my hand tighter. She wouldn't blame me for his death, even if I did. She nodded one more time, then turned to her daughter-in-law and held her close.

But her words were directed to me. "Tell me how it happened, Andy. I need to know."

By the time I finished, Em had joined us, along with Rick, Miguel, Alice, and Jane's kids.

"Rick told me all about it," Em said, hugging me again, then Jane, then Gladys. "I'm so sorry about Bill, Gladys. I don't know if it helps, but Rick says that Bill was the real hero. He threw himself out of a tree to draw their fire."

Gladys wiped her tears on an handkerchief, then blew her nose loudly.

"Of course he was, the crazy old coot. Always knew he would die like a cowboy, with his six-guns on." She looked at me. "He did, didn't he?"

"He did."

"His pearl-handled revolvers...crazy old man...God, how I loved that cowboy...."

159

"Oh, Gladys!" Jane buried her face in Gladys' bosom.

"That's alright, darlin'. He did what he had to do. We can be grateful he made it all come out as good as it did. I know he's happy about that. He loved his Danny Boy more 'n life itself."

A more fitting epitaph would never be written. Wild Bill would agree.

There's a nice fish and chips place on the spit, and after eating we drove back to Port Angeles to visit Dan Junior in the hospital. Our dinner had felt a little like a celebration, but it was more of an early wake for a missing guest of honor. Bill would have enjoyed it. Somewhere, he was raising his flask on high, acknowledging the toasts to himself.

We took two cars to Port Angeles. Marilyn Hensel piloted her Eurovan, conveying Alice, Miguel, and the Crawford clan. Em, Rick and I took the Blazer.

Sometimes, people who are very close can communicate without having to resort to that imprecise approximation we call language. It was like that for the three of us that night. I drove most of the way without talking, and Em and Rick were equally silent. Once in awhile Em would pat my knee. Occasionally, Rick would lean forward from the back seat and grip our shoulders. Most of the time we just rode along quietly, feeling close, grateful to be alive, overjoyed to be together.

Except I kept reliving the whole damn movie, frame by bloody frame, with slo-mo examination of the highlights. Wild Bill showing me the weapons, telling me where to aim, providing the reassurance I needed by assuming I would do what was needed. Hefting the H&K machine pistol for the first time, surprised at its light weight, more surprised by how normal it felt by the time the kidnappers arrived. Swallowing the wonderful burn of the scotch in Wild Bill's flask.

"Think of them as animals," Wild Bill had counseled. I'd refined that to rabid hyenas, untamable mad dogs—literally—feeding in a pack.

Rick leaned forward and wrapped a lanky arm around my neck, pulled himself close, and whispered in my ear. "Those guys were sick, dad. They enjoyed castrating that dog. They laughed, dad, they actually laughed, when two of them told us about shooting Dan's dad after they cut off his ear. They giggled when they cut off Dan Junior's arm. I knew they were going to kill us after they got that micro... micro…fiche? I know, 'cause I heard them talking about where to put the bodies. Our bodies."

Then he sat back and leaned into his own recollections. In a moment, he spoke again, clearly and strongly.

"They deserved to die. I'm glad they're dead. They were animals. Dirty, fucking animals. Worse than animals, because animals don't kill each other for fun."

I could only nod my head. Em moved closer and patted my knee some more.

"But dad?"

"Yeah?"

"I think I want to keep our guns locked up for awhile, okay?"

My eyes filled with tears. "Yeah," I said. "I can handle that."

When we reached the hospital, I dropped Em and Rick at the main entrance, then circled the lot, looking for a parking place. When I finally found one I sat there for a few minutes, letting all that had happened roll over me. I mopped my face with my handkerchief, then walked slowly across the lot to the hospital.

27

Dan Junior was still groggy, but alert enough to recognize us. He tried to smile. The effort wore him out and his eyes closed. We waited a few more minutes, then said our goodbyes to Mommie Dearest, who remained at bedside.

From the hospital, I called Jack Alford, the Bainbridge cop. He passed along two messages, one from Tom MacDonald, the other from none other than an executive vice president at Boeing. I figured Tom MacDonald was calling to thank me for the microfiche and aiding his quest for a Pulitzer. I figured the Boeing veep was calling to negotiate some kind of damage control settlement. I called him first.

The guy's name was…well, let's just call him Jones. One should protect the innocent until proven guilty, right? So we'll call him Jones.

"Congratulations on rescuing the children, Mister Eastman," he said.

"Doesn't that leave a bad taste in your mouth, saying that?"

"I know what you are driving at Mister Eastman, but believe me, you couldn't be more mistaken."

"I see. So you still maintain that Boeing is an innocent party?"

"Of course. We're as much a victim in this whole conspiracy as you have been. I figured you'd understand that by now."

"Indeed I do. I know all about Boeing's extortion scheme, how long it's been going on, and that Boeing is responsible for kidnappings and murders. And tomorrow, the whole damned world will know it as well."

Jones sighed, sounding more sad than worried. Actually, more like an infinitely patient parent, operating near his breaking point.

"I take it you have not actually seen the microfiches."

"I've seen them. I've had them in my hand. But no, I haven't read them on a viewer."

"Then you need to do so. Immediately. Then, together, perhaps we can figure out how to minimize the damage that's already been done. I will meet the noon ferry from Winslow tomorrow when it docks in Seattle. Try to be on it."

Jesus. What was on those microfiches?

"Are you still there, Mr. Eastman?"

"Yeah."

"Then look at the microfiches. Do that, for your sake, not mine. Unless I hear otherwise from you in the morning, I'll meet you when you get off the noon ferry to Seattle."

I yielded.

"On one condition, Jones."

"Yes?"

"That Tom MacDonald of the *Seattle Times* joins us."

There was a short silence, then, "Yes. That's a very good idea."

Jones' self-assurance bothered me. I thought he would crumble when I mentioned the press. But maybe he planned to buy off Mac-Donald, too.

When I called MacDonald, at least he behaved as I expected. Partly, anyway. He thanked me for the exclusive interview and said he'd look forward to meeting with me and Boeing's Jones tomorrow. Then he asked about the microfiches, which he had not yet received.

"I wouldn't bother you, Mister Eastman, but I'm coming up on deadline."

I told him I didn't know what had happened to the microfiches, but I would get them to him as soon as I could.

So I called my printer, Dale Kennedy. Dale didn't answer right away, and for a moment the thought crossed my mind that he had finally sold out and given the microfiche to a much higher bidder: Boeing. Was that why Jones had sounded so sure of himself? Because he had the only copy of the microfiche in his own hot little hands? But that didn't make any sense. He'd just insisted that I should read them.

My quandary was interrupted when Dale finally answered. He sounded so panicky that I was a little ashamed of doubting his anti-establishment convictions.

"Thank God! I've been trying to reach you all night. The cop at the Captain's House wouldn't say where you were. Jesus, Andy, we're in trouble. Those microfiches aren't at all what you said they were. You gotta see them right away. I didn't send them to the newspaper, like you wanted."

"You still have them?" Not all my suspicion had evaporated.

"Of course. I figured I better hold onto them until you had a chance to read them. When can you get here?"

"What is it, Dale? What's on them?"

"I don't think we should talk about it over the phone."

Much as I wanted to, this time I couldn't attribute Dale's long-standing paranoia about tapped phones to his coming of age in the era of the Pentagon papers. He sounded genuinely worried, if not panicky. I told him I would be there first thing in the morning. Then I called MacDonald and told him to put his scoop on hold until we had met with Boeing's Executive VP Jones. "Something's come up," I said.

MacDonald wasn't happy about the delay, but he agreed. What choice did he have?

All of us spent the night at Gladys Crawford's place in Sequim. Early the next morning I drove to the island alone.

"Thank God," Dale Kennedy said. "I was afraid someone would come and get these in the night."

He turned on the microfiche viewer. It didn't take long to see why Executive VP Jones had sounded the way he did. The first thing I did was to call Tom MacDonald. I told him his big scoop would be substantially different than anticipated. He wanted details. I told him he would get the whole story at one o'clock, directly from Boeing and from printouts of the microfiches themselves. MacDonald said he would call Jones and confirm the meeting.

Dale made two hard-copy enlargements of the microfiches, one for me, one for MacDonald. While Dale made the copies, I called Garfield Gatsby and told him to call off the suit. He refused to, unless I told him why. So I did, briefly, then told him that he was still my lawyer, and he would be in big trouble if he didn't do as I wanted. "Cancel the god-damned suit!"

"Okay, okay. I'll cancel it. But you do realize that...."

"I know. It'll cost me. And I'll be wide open to all kinds of counter-suits too, right?"

"Just so you know."

"That's the least of my worries at the moment."

"Very well, then." He did remember to congratulate me on the boy's rescue before hanging up, and I thanked him for the thought.

Then I thanked Dale, more profusely, for having the wit to disobey my instructions.

"Put your money where your thankful mouth is, Andy. And where my hungry mouth is."

"Streamliner Diner?"

After breakfast with Dale, I walked two blocks to the Winslow ferry terminal and caught the 12:10 boat to Seattle, not quite ready for my meeting with Jones and MacDonald. The queasy feeling in my stomach had nothing to do with the Streamliner's food, for I hadn't eaten anything. I couldn't attribute it to sea-sickness, either; Puget Sound was as smooth as glass.

Jones was waiting for me in front of the terminal, behind the wheel of a newer Mercedes wagon. Tom MacDonald stood alongside the car.

The Norton Building and its subterranean parking garage was a short two-block ride from the ferry terminal. From the garage we rose in the elevator to the Harbor Club on the top floor, where we were ushered to a small private room furnished with a single table set for three. An erasable white board and several colored markers stood on a nearby easel.

A waiter brought us drinks and I handed each man a copy of the microfiche print-outs. Jones nodded as he read; no surprises there for him. Tom MacDonald, on the other hand, whistled several tuneless little ditties as he read. Our food arrived as they finished reading.

"Gentlemen, let's eat first," Jones said. "It's going to be a long afternoon."

After our lunch—I have no recollection of what we ate—we talked briefly about culpability: mine, Dan Crawford's, Boeing's, and the press, and we handled that relatively quickly. I wanted to be self-righteously indignant, but I couldn't. Dan Crawford had taken me in completely. I was at fault for trusting him. There's nothing wrong with trusting your friends. But I had been way too ready to believe his story about corporate corruption and the greed of senior government employees; apparently, I wanted to believe in that particular conspiracy. Obviously, I *needed* to believe; I had been a willing dupe.

Dan had been right about two elements: there had been a conspiracy, and it had benefitted Boeing; they'd gotten government contracts they otherwise might not have received if the playing field had been level. So Boeing was culpable. But the conspiracy itself was hatched by Dan, and it had continued for years without Boeing's awareness. He'd been a trusted employee and he'd led them down the garden path. Still, Boeing was liable because Dan was their employee.

As for the news media, represented in our meeting by Tom MacDonald of the *Seattle Times*, their victimhood was fairly obvious. They'd just reported the news they gathered, much of it from me. It wasn't their fault that information wasn't entirely accurate. From a media perspective, their principle concern now was getting it right, reporting things precisely from here on out, the chips falling where they may.

But to MacDonald's credit, he saw how premature full disclosure of all of the facts could compound the damage already done—to individuals like me and my family, to Mommie Dearest and her family, to corporations like Boeing, and to institutions like the FBI and the military services. So he agreed to cooperate, so long as he wasn't asked to "spin" the truth into oblivion.

The question then became, how could we do that?

See, here was the problem: Dan Crawford's microfiches told a much different tale than the story Dan had told me, and it was no wonder he had taken such pains to protect that tale from exposure. He had invested seven years in creating those filmed records, and they were indeed full of damning information, the publication of which would be devastating to nearly everyone whose name was mentioned.

The microfiches *did* list extortion targets—that much of what Dan told me was true. And the list did contain "the goods" on a long list of men and women of middling to great power, men and women who had varying degrees of influence in awarding government contracts.

In his conversations with me, Dan had omitted one important fact. True, Boeing had won contracts as a result of Dan's list, but it wasn't Boeing's list. It was Dan Crawford's list, Dan's list entirely. He had used his position at Boeing to gather information, but he had done so without the company's knowledge or sanction. As he had uncovered bits of incriminating information, he hired private investigators to discover more, paying those operatives out of Boeing funds that he controlled and manipulated. Those Boeing funds were legitimate; they were "entertainment" and "competitive research" funds that were to be used to wine and dine existing clients and potential customers, and to gather information about competitors. All legitimate company funds, to be used for legitimate business purposes—and all perfectly legal. But how Dan had actually used those funds was not.

At first, Dan had spent only a few thousand dollars to pay just a few researchers and investigators. As he then adroitly used the information his investigators had collected, he was able to supplement Boeing's "kitty" by blackmailing a few of the principals involved. Some of those blackmail receipts were used to pay back the Boeing entertainment and research funds, but most of those illicitly gotten gains went into numbered Caribbean accounts in Dan's name. One of the microfiched records contained copies of semi-annual statements of those account, now totaling well into seven figures.

Other microfiched pages recorded his legitimate expenses; others, the illegitimate expenses of his profitable venture: mostly cash payments to his own network of information gatherers. Call them spies, or agents.

Most of the rest of the microfiches contained terse and often titillating summaries of the "ammunition" his agents had gathered, elucidated in page after page of letters Crawford had sent to his "clients," letters that also provided terse instructions on paying his "fee."

It was fascinating reading, and I found myself wondering what had driven him to want to immortalize such incriminating evidence. I'll never know for sure, but I suspect it was his habit as a lawyer to document everything, his way keeping track of his business.

Many of Dan Crawford's "clients" lived outside of the U.S. More than a few were high-level ministers in various world capitols. A few were scions of royal families in middle eastern countries, defacto directors of family-owned companies in family-run countries, countries always in the market for the latest in aerospace and anti-terrorist technology.

It was in one of those countries where Dan Crawford finally had over-reached himself and some of those "clients" had struck back directly, notifying the U.S. State Department, who passed the information on to the FBI and the CIA. A few others had taken a more direct approach, hiring mercenaries, many of whom had a history of working both sides of the fence: current and former FBI agents and CIA operatives. Free-lance investigators. Kidnappers. Killers.

Two of them were familiar to me: FBI Special Agents who were listed in a "memo for the files": Special Agents Doorham and Griffin, both of whom had provided information to Dan and then become blackmailed clients themselves, forced to provide more and more incriminating information on others.

Crawford's scheme had begun unraveling about fifteen months ago, after he tried to blackmail a certain prince in a very hot desert kingdom friendly to the United States. Commander Bottoms of the US Coast Guard had been Crawford's unwitting intermediary with the prince. Bottoms had been sent to the Arabian Gulf to demonstrate the potential of an updated high-speed jet-foil boat similar to one that Boeing had manufactured in the 1960's. At Crawford's request, Bottoms carried a letter from Crawford to the prince. The letter was in a sealed Boeing envelope, and Bottoms assumed it was an official proposal from Boeing. Commander Bottoms knew the prince had been charged with the responsibility to upgrade his country's fledgling navy.

After opening the envelope and reading Crawford's demands, the prince assumed Commander Bottoms was in on the deal. He dismissed the Coast Guard officer without so much as a parting *Salaam*, which probably perplexed Bottoms, who had thought he had behaved with the utmost propriety. The prince didn't do anything right away. He let his anger seethe for more than a year before arranging to have Bottoms accidentally drowned. He had taken his time, but he had killed the messenger, and Dan Crawford had gotten the message that the originator of the insulting message—Dan Crawford—would be next.

Judging by Crawford's accelerated rate of collections in the last few months, he had been trying to get as much money together as he could, while he still could. His memos to the file testified to his growing terror. It was obvious that he was trying to find some way to use the information in his files, perhaps negotiating a final settlement that would buy himself and his family a safe exile or maybe just to buy off his tormentors—the very people he had been tormenting.

But four hired guns had gotten to him first, kidnapping his son and Rick and Miguel, when it became apparent that I must be helping Dan Crawford. Finally, when Dan refused to give up his bargaining chips, he had been killed.

As we sorted through the detritus of Dan Crawford's dereliction, Boeing's Jones and the *Times'* MacDonald and I concluded that we would not worry, at least not unduly, about the FBI. That agency's credibility was not particularly high anyway, and exposure of a few more turn-coat agents wouldn't cause much additional damage. After the quadruple debacle of Hoover excesses, Watergate cover-ups, and

Branch Davidian and Ruby Ridge massacres, the FBI would survive this smelly but relatively small fart in a whirlwind.

I did insist, however, that MacDonald make it clear in his reporting that Special Agent Chester Arthur Griffin had sought to make things right, even though doing so would end his career with the FBI. And that he had been killed for his efforts. MacDonald vowed to do his best.

The Boeing Company, on the other hand, was going to take it in the shorts. There was no way to get around the fact that Dan Crawford had been one of their chief negotiators. That he had acted in their name would badly tarnish the company's reputation.

There was no way around that. Boeing had indeed benefited from Dan Crawford's activities, even though they had not sanctioned his methods. The publicity would deliver a blow to the company's reputation—and its business—possibly for years. Government contracts would be cancelled or, at best, renegotiated and delayed. That would hurt enough. But for Boeing, that was comparatively small potatoes.

More serious was the fact that many of Crawford's victims were current and future commercial airplane customers. If this whole sordid mess wasn't handled properly, billions of dollars of airliner orders would go to Airbus Industrie by default.

Some of the damage had already been ameliorated by letters from Boeing's corporate offices—personal apologies from the CEO to victims of Dan Crawford's extortion. But for some of the people involved—hell, for some of the nations involved—any contact from Boeing, even returning funds extorted by Dan Crawford, would be viewed as a further insult, an even more egregious invasion of privacy, but worst of all, would threaten the legitimacy of those family dynasties that portrayed themselves as benevolent benefactors of the citizens they ruled.

At the end of that very long day, we concluded we needed to publicize Dan Crawford's activities fully, but not name the specific individuals he targeted for extortion, nor would we provide dates or places that would identify Dan's victims.

Tom MacDonald would head that effort. He would make the extortion scheme public, while stressing that The Boeing Company itself had not created the scheme. That would be a small start at damage control. I, of course, would withdraw my suit, with the lame excuse that it was based on lies told by Dan Crawford.

That wouldn't be enough, we knew. Boeing's core business would still be at risk. The company employed so many people, almost 70,000 in Seattle alone, that any decline in its reputation would be followed immediately by a plunge in sales, commercial as well as military, and grave damage to the company, its employees, and its supplier's employees. Many completely innocent people would suffer.

So we talked and we talked, without coming up with much more we could do, until I hit on what would be, pardon the pun, a novel solution.

"I'll write a book that tells the whole story."

MacDonald and Jones both laughed. "Aw, come on. Who would believe it?" They weren't speaking figuratively; they really wanted to know: who *would* believe it?

"Maybe no one," I said. "But how else are you going to tell the complete story without everybody dismissing it as corporate propaganda and part of a continuing cover-up?"

Jones said, "It'll never work. There's got to be another way."

I said, "Look. Sometimes people are more likely to believe truth when it is presented as fiction. That's just the way folks are. Maybe because their guard is down or they're more receptive when they're also being entertained.

But readers can't be fooled completely; that's why good novels have to be more realistic—more believable—than real life. Trust me," I said, "I've got more than enough information to make this a realistic story."

"In fact," I continued, "I'll bet that most people will believe that it's all true. Remember that most of what will be in the book is entirely factual and much of it has already been seen on TV and read about in the papers: the kidnapping, my house and Mommie Dearest's house being blown up, the shootout...."

"Mommie Dearest?" VP Jones asked. "Who's Mommie Dearest?"

"Jane Crawford," I said. "'*Crawford.*' Get it? Like Joan Crawford? Never mind. You'll understand when you read the book."

I added one more thing, more or less thinking aloud. "The book will be published as fiction, okay? There will be the usual upfront disclaimer saying it's a work of imagination that includes elements of fact. If I word that disclaimer just right, readers will be assume that the disclaimer is a mere formality, and they'll be incline to think the whole story is true. I tell you, it's a can't-lose proposition, fellas."

"Sounds like you're going to write about this, regardless of what we decide," Jones said.

"I might as well. I've dropped my suit, I've already quit my day job at Boeing, and I have a contract to write a book anyway. It might as well be this one."

"You already have a publisher?" MacDonald said.

"Wallingford Press," I said. "And my editor, Chris Noble, already thinks I'm Hemingway reincarnate." Well, he didn't, not really. But hey, I needed to be persuasive. I could see McDonald and Jones were wavering.

"Hold on," I said, fishing my cell phone out of my pants pocket and Chris Noble's card out of my wallet. As I waited for the call to connect, I remember thinking: hey, these cell phone thingies might just catch on.

I caught Chris Noble at his desk, working late. First thing he did was to apologize for not calling me when he read about my son being kidnapped—a story that had appeared in the *New York Times* when our house was blown up. I thanked him, then broached the idea for the story. It took very little persuasion to get him to agree to publish this new story first, provided I could get it written while interest was high.

Then I handed the phone to Tom MacDonald, who listened for awhile, then passed the phone along to Boeing VP Jones. Noble confirmed to both of them that Wallingford Press would indeed publish the "novel" as quickly as I could write it. Noble added that Wallingford would start their advertising campaign immediately, with a focus on connecting with cable TV commentators and placing display ads in selected newspapers—especially the *Seattle Times*—for the book.

Tom MacDonald was won over immediately; he'd not only see his name under every article he wrote for the paper, he'd also get strokes from the paper's advertising folks.

Jones agreed. "All right," he said. "Let's do it. What could it hurt?"

So, there you have it. I wrote the book, it's been published, and Boeing is still making a bunch of airplanes. I guess it all worked out okay. But then I had an easier job than Hemingway did.

He had to make up his stories.

Postscript

Three months have passed, and I wish I could say that everything worked out as well for all of us as it seems to be working out for Boeing. For me, once the publicity died down, life went back to normal, more or less. I'm not at Boeing any more, but I am finishing up the stories that Wallingford originally bought. One will be released next year, and the second a year later. Wallingford expects both of them to do well.

When the dust settles, I probably will be make more money as a free-lance writer than I did at Boeing, but now we have to buy our own health insurance. I can work on my own schedule and don't have to commute by ferry to work every day, so that's a plus. Although, truth be told, sometimes I miss the commute and find myself taking round-trips on the boat, making notes on my new iBook G3 laptop.

Rick has made a good recovery from the trauma of the kidnapping and the rescue, though he had trouble sleeping for a month or so. Attending Wild Bill's funeral and giving a eulogy extolling the old rancher's heroism seemed to help him more than anything, even more than the psychologist he's been seeing. But Rick's a different kid than he was just a few months ago, and it has nothing to do with being a few months older. Unlike most of his compatriots, Rick has an acute sense of his own mortality, and a greatly enhanced grasp of the fragility and value of life. That's good, I suppose, but I feel like I've stolen the last years of his childhood.

On his own, and without telling me, Rick put his .22 rifle and revolver on consignment with a gun dealer in Poulsbo. He says he's saving up for his first car. This summer he's working full-time at an espresso stand in Seattle and adding more dollars to that fund. I've agreed to match whatever he put in his savings account, and it looks like Em and I will be experiencing a more typical kind of terror in a couple months when he starts driving.

Miguel Sharp bounced back more quickly and wrote a book about his experiences that, so far, has sold twice as many copies as mine, probably because his wasn't "fiction." It looks like Miguel will achieve millionaire status on his own, long before he inherits that status.

Dan Crawford Junior hasn't fared so well. He nearly died following an allergic reaction to antibiotics at the hospital. That setback, plus the physical and emotional damage he suffered in captivity, plus the awful knowledge of his father's misdeeds, seems to be more than he can handle right now. But I understand he's still in intensive psychiatric therapy, and we're all hopeful. Please, God. Give DJ his life back.

We haven't seen Mommie Dearest much, not since a month ago, when Jane said they were moving. Last week, we heard through the grapevine they had already moved, but no one knows where they went. I suspect Mommie Dearest and Dan Junior prefer it that way, and maybe a fresh start in a new locale isn't such a bad idea.

Gladys Crawford, Wild Bill's widow, died quietly a little over a month ago—cardiac arrest while sleeping. Em, Rick, Alice, Miguel, and I went to her funeral, along with nearly everyone in Sequim. That was the last place we saw Mommie Dearest and Dan Junior. They were polite but distant. I figured they were zoned out pharmacologically. But I know that's not all it was.

For now, Em and I remain together. At the moment, we're renting a two-bedroom apartment in Winslow. Meanwhile, the insurance settlement for our house sits in a joint savings account until we figure out what to do. We're holding off making a decision about a new house until we're sure we'll continue to be a couple.

Two weeks after the shootout, we finally were able to talk about our abbreviated separation. It was a good, productive discussion, and we're having more of those discussions now. They're always painful, but they're always authentic too, honest and open. I have to think that's good.

Em *is* immensely grateful that Rick survived but she's angry that I was so easily taken in by Dan—and she's furious that I kept so many secrets from her. My violent solution to the kidnapping, oddly enough, doesn't seem to bother her much. It bothers me more, probably because it was my dereliction that had led to the boys' being kidnapped in the first place. I'll always struggle with that.

The good news is that both Em and I are, for now, committed to giving our marriage another try. We don't argue about money at all now. I'm not sure why, but I think it's because I've finally disproven her mother's constant harangue that I'll never amount to anything, never be able to send Rick to an Ivy League school, yada, yada, yada. I can't be certain that's the reason, but I do know that neither Em nor I talk to her mother much anymore. I don't miss the old bag. I think Em feels the same way.

I think both of us realize that we have weathered the worst that any two people could experience. And I know that we're both grateful that Rick is alive and is doing okay.

That has to count for something, doesn't it?

About the Author

Dennis Berry's career as a writer includes stints with the U.S. Forest Service, the U.S. Army Corps of Engineers, architecture and engineering firms in the Pacific Northwest, the Royal Saudi Navy and the Saudi Aramco oil company in the Kingdom of Saudi Arabia, and The Boeing Company in Seattle. Journalism credits include feature articles for *The Daily Astorian* in Astoria, Oregon and *The Chinook Observer* in Long Beach, Washington.

Works of fiction, besides *Mommie Dearest,* include *Eye Wit,* a mystery written with Hazel Dawkins and *Papa Doc,* another Andy Eastman novel (publication date: May 2012).

Dennis enjoys life with a diminutive yet stalwart badger hound in Oregon's tsunami zone near the mouth of the mighty Columbia River.

Contact him at:

http://www.murderprose.com and http://www.dennis-berry.com.

Made in the USA
Charleston, SC
23 September 2011